THE
WEREWOLF
MURDERS

THE
WEREWOLF
MURDERS

A Niccolo Benedetti Mystery

WILLIAM L. DEANDREA

A PERFECT CRIME BOOK
DOUBLEDAY
NEW YORK LONDON TORONTO SYDNEY AUCKLAND

A Perfect Crime Book
PUBLISHED BY DOUBLEDAY
a division of Bantam Doubleday Dell Publishing Group, Inc.
666 Fifth Avenue, New York, New York 10103

DOUBLEDAY is a trademark of Doubleday, a division of
Bantam Doubleday Dell Publishing Group, Inc.

BOOK DESIGN BY TASHA HALL

Library of Congress Cataloging-in-Publication Data
DeAndrea, William L.
The werewolf murders : a Niccolo Benedetti mystery / by William L.
DeAndrea.
p.   cm.
"A Perfect Crime book."
I. Title.
PS3554.E174W47   1992
813'.54—dc20   91-44676
                                                                  CIP

ISBN 0-385-42089-7

1   3   5   7   9   10   8   6   4   2

First Edition

*To Gay Martinolich,
World's greatest and most
patient pen pal*

THE
WEREWOLF
MURDERS

1

The Olympique Scientifique Internationale was an idea of self-conscious magnificence. It was grandiose, and hugely impractical.

Only a Frenchman could have conceived of it, thought Paul Levesque when the baron first broached the idea. Only, in fact, a Frenchman of a specific type. The baron's type. A type that hardly existed any more.

Baron Pierre Benac was a small, round man with a deep voice which he cultivated each morning with a set of vocal exercises. It was the baron's belief that the orders of large men with large voices were most readily obeyed. Since it was his fate to be small, he would do his utmost to maximize the effect of his voice. Levesque, as the baron's private secretary and chief aide, was the only person in the world to whom the baron had entrusted this confidence.

And there must have been something to it, Levesque reflected, because the baron claimed grandiosity and impracticality as a birthright. An ancestor had been ennobled by the emperor Napoleon when he had conceived and carried out a plan to sink a British man-o'-war by firing at it from the shore with one sixteen-pound cannon and six muskets.

More than any of the barons who had come between,

Pierre Benac possessed the spirit and drive of his ancestor. The current baron's inspirations (and Levesque thanked God for this) ran more to building or achieving things than to destroying them. His love was France, a France that was the beacon and glory of the world, and that love was boundless.

The truly amazing thing, Levesque reflected, was how often the baron's grandiose plans *worked.* The octopus farm in the Mediterranean. The computer analysis of the Cathedral of Notre-Dame, so that it might be rebuilt if ever damaged or destroyed by some catastrophe. Even the necklace of reflecting satellites to celebrate the one hundredth anniversary of the Eiffel Tower would have worked, if astronomers around the world hadn't protested that the extra light in the sky would make it impossible for them to do their work.

When questioned about this, the baron would clear his throat and explain, "The motto of my family is: 'A man with dreams can achieve anything.' How much more, then, can a man achieve who has both dreams and a large fortune?"

And so, in the waning years of the twentieth century, with the world's dictatorships and repressive governments falling like autumn leaves, he saw the human spirit poised to soar to heights never before reached, and the baron dreamed his latest and greatest dream.

"Paul," he said one morning at the office as Levesque tried in vain to induce the baron to look at some octopus production reports, "I must be part of this. I must—*France* must—do something to mark this as the start of a new era. We must do something to make concrete for the world the potential for greatness in Man that has recently been unlocked!"

Levesque looked at the baron's pointed beard, quivering with excitement, and knew he was in for trouble.

And so was born l'Olympique Scientifique Internationale, or as it came to be known, OSI. "What de Coubertin did for the body, I shall do for the mind. I shall gather the greatest scientific minds in the world, and bring them together to share their knowledge and to spur each other to great achievements.

"And *you,* you my dear friend, shall organize it for me."

Levesque had seen this coming. Though he knew it was useless, he tried to wiggle out. "Monsieur le Baron, where can we do this?"

The baron stroked his shiny black moustaches and frowned. Then he snapped his fingers. "Simply the most beautiful and peaceful spot on earth—Mont-St.-Denis."

Mont-St.-Denis was one of the baron's many holdings, a ski resort as fashionable as Cortina or Gstaad, if less well known. The baron fell in love with the idea; in the end, it made Levesque's job easier, since the baron was not afraid to back his mad fancies without limit. It was to cost the baron many millions of francs to turn the ski resort into a dream laboratory for some two hundred scientists, and many more to induce them to come.

To say nothing, of course, of the lost skiing revenue. "The townspeople will not suffer," the baron declared. And that was that.

It took the better part of two years, but at last the remodeling had been done, the equipment had been installed, the diplomatic hurdles (even in a world largely at peace, there are diplomatic hurdles) had been cleared, the scientists had arrived, and l'Olympique Scientifique Internationale was ready to begin.

The opening ceremonies were the happiest day of the baron's life. He had been warned that the scientists would not care for such dashing and romantic goings-on, but Pierre Benac had known better. Scientists they were, committed to order and rationality, yes, but they were still men and women of flesh and blood. More. They were the modern counterparts of the Columbuses, the Magellans, the Champlains. The explorers, the leaders into new lands. That they no longer needed to risk their very lives to do so was immaterial; the spirit of adventure (and the desire for glory) *must* be the same.

And so it seemed. On the great day, there were bands and balloons and doves, and the lighting of a flame. The media of the world had gathered, and the festivities were shown on live television to all parts of the earth.

Each of the two hundred six participating scientists was introduced by name and nation and field of expertise. Each walked to a podium to stirring music. Each received a handshake, a gold medal, and an accolade from the baron. Some beamed; some were solemn. All, the baron knew, were touched and proud, but none more so than Pierre Benac himself. He knew he had done something few men can achieve—he had consciously and deliberately made History.

And while the baron didn't disdain any glory that might come to him personally, his greatest joy was that he had wrought l'Olympique Scientifique Internationale for the glory of mankind.

Levesque would always remember the baron on that day with a mixture of pride and sadness. It *was* a great achievement. The fact that it was to turn into a grinding nightmare of superstition and fear and death was not the baron's fault.

2

She always did her running at the first light of dawn. It was the perfect antidote to a long night's work. Back in New Mexico (she'd lived there for six years, now, but she never thought of it as "back *home*"), she would simply run the four miles down the mountainside when the sky got too bright for good seeing. Then she'd take a shower, have breakfast, and go to sleep.

That wouldn't work here. For one thing, her room in the Hotel de Leone was separated by a steep mountainside and a craggy valley from the observatory Baron Benac had built up above the top of the ski run on Mont-St.-Denis. For another thing, the observatory was closed tonight—the nova wouldn't be visible. Too much other light in the sky.

Dr. Karin Tebner hadn't been the first to see the nova. If she had been, she'd be famous, or at least as famous as an eyeball astronomer can get in these days of X-ray analysis and radioastronomy.

Still, Karin believed there was something about taking actual pictures of the heavens and studying them, or even giving into the atavistic urge to put your face right up to the eyepiece and look at the ancient light from distant stars, that no amount of computer readouts could replace.

Of course, the electronic astronomers got to work regular hours—the radio data is always there no matter what bright object is in the sky. Nor did the techie types have to be where the instruments were. Willem Bork, for instance, was working on data that came to him daily via satellite from the Arecibo dish in Puerto Rico.

Bork was here, as Karin was, as all the scientists were, she supposed, more for the honor of the thing than in the expectation of getting any serious work done.

Well, Karin told herself, you're certainly not getting any work done lying in bed reading a horror novel. Not even your running.

It was always like this on her nights off. Since they came bunched together once a month, it was always a temptation to go native, to adjust herself to days-awake, nights-asleep instead of the late-afternoon-till-dawn routine she needed to follow for her work.

Once or twice, she had given into the temptation and had regretted it. She walked around in a daze for a week before she got readjusted.

Karin threw her legs over the side of the bed. She pulled off her pajamas, then put on her running bra, a pair of cotton panties, and some sweats. She accepted her body and her looks without loving them. She wasn't tall or especially shapely, but she'd do. She'd given up hating her freckles. She was pleased with her natural strawberry-blond hair. She knew she looked a lot younger than her thirty-two years. This sometimes proved irksome *("Doctor* Tebner? But you don't look old enough to be out of *high school!"),* but Karin knew a lot of women worked very hard to be taken for younger than they were.

Of course, she reflected as she laced on her sneakers, pluses and minuses were all pretty academic when your work precluded a social life of any sort.

Karin put her keys, passport, and OSI identification

card (the photograph on which made her look twelve) into the pocket across the belly of her sweatshirt and zipped it up. Then she pulled the hood up over her head, tied the string under her chin, and left.

The night clerk at the hotel, a skinny old man named Claude, grinned at her as she went out. Claude thought they were sharing some huge secret. She had tried to explain running for fitness to him, but her high-school French and Claude's tourist-trap English ("You leave a note for the manager, no?") had proven inadequate to the task. Claude drew his own conclusion—she was sneaking out in disguise early every morning to meet a lover. The fact that she came back each day sweaty and flushed only added to his conviction.

It was early June, but she could see her breath in the predawn light. The altitude explained the chill, of course, and the fact that the higher up you were, the farther over the horizon you could see. Therefore sunrise came much earlier, and took longer to take the chill out of the thin air. People had told her that by noontime it would be quite pleasant, but Karin was never awake at noon to know.

She didn't mind the cold. She followed her usual route —away from town and out toward the ski lodge, near the base of the funicular she and her colleagues rode to work every day, then back along the north road on the edge of town, curving around until she reached the Boulevard de Ville, (or, as she liked to think of it, Main Street) and back to the hotel.

Today she thought about luck. A very unscientific concept, luck. As a scientist, she should realize that if you could simply quantify the factors involved, what looked like luck would be the simple workings of the laws of probability. And she did know that. But she still believed in luck.

All right, the laws of probability said that supernovas would occur at irregular intervals; that there was nothing remarkable in the fact that after a drought of over a thousand years, there should appear two in one decade, the first visible from the Southern Hemisphere, and the second in the Northern Hemisphere, as though in the interests of fairness.

Neither of the new supernovas was in our galaxy, naturally. If they had been, no telescopes would have been needed. Like the one the Chinese had recorded all those years ago, it would have been visible in the daytime to the naked eye, and might have caused people to cast a second shadow. It was still a fairly remarkable occurrence, all the more so since it had happened again so recently after a delay of centuries. Karin felt lucky to have been in on it.

Not as lucky as Dr. Goetz, who had first spotted the new light on the blinker, but lucky enough.

Baron Benac must have been feeling pretty lucky, too. Karin puffed breath through a smile as she ran. The baron was such a sweet, charming little man. He was the first, and so far only, man ever to have kissed the hand of Karin Tebner, Ph.D., and he did it as if it were her due, as if she were a duchess or something. She'd treasure the memory.

So she was glad things were working out so well for him. OSI had started in late April (to let the townspeople get the skiing season in, Karin supposed) and would run until next April. And already, in less than six weeks, the inmates at the baron's little scientific asylum were coming up with results. There was Dr. Goetz and the supernova. There were the geneticists, a Filipino and a Kenyan, who had compared notes and realized they'd each already done about half the work toward preventing the anopheles mosquito from mating, big news for those parts of the world where malaria was still a problem. And that American on leave from Monsanto teaming up with the Frenchman (she could still see the baron's beaming face in the local paper) to cook up a new fiber many times stronger than steel, but lighter and finer than silk.

That last one might have all sorts of ramifications. Bullet-proof clothes that didn't weigh a ton. More finely calibrated optical equipment. Stockings that never ran. Nah —if the material was that tough, it would probably cut your toes.

By the time the north road looped around to join Main Street, Karin's muscles were warm and loose, and she was ready to pick up the pace. It was just as well to run faster through town because by the time she got there, smells of baking would begin to fill the air.

One day, back in April, she had occupied her mind by doing a little statistical breakdown on the town of Mont-St.-Denis. She had worked it out that there was a *pâtisserie* every 1.67 blocks along Main Street, and a *charcuterie* every 3.01. They all got busy preparing their wares for the day about the time she started running. Since her two major culinary weaknesses were pastry (or the long loaves of French bread that were as good as pastry) and delicatessen food, the run down the Boulevard de Ville each morning was a greater test of her self-discipline than the running itself could ever be.

There was an especially strong scent this morning. Perhaps Belanger et Cie, her favorite *charcuterie,* was roasting a pig, or doing a batch of those absolutely marvelous, slightly charred sausages.

Stop it, Tebner, she ordered herself. You'll talk yourself into a pig-out breakfast again. Karin frequently gave herself orders. She obeyed much less frequently.

She ran past Belanger, and the smell was stronger yet. Odd, but not unpleasant. She put it from her mind.

There were fewer shops here as she approached the town square, renamed, as part of the opening ceremonies that had been held there, Place de Science. Karin looked for the Eternal Flame, an aluminum thing like an art deco barbecue grill about eight feet high. The Torch of Science was almost exactly a half mile from the hotel. As soon as she passed it, she'd begin her sprint. Scientist or not, Karin was unable to give up the English system of measurements in her personal life.

She saw the flame at last. It was a lot smaller than usual, and pretty smoky. The baron would have to tell somebody to mix more oxygen in with the gas, or clean the jet or something.

Karin reached the square. When she looked at the torch, she stopped in her tracks. Her brain was suddenly so full, she couldn't remember to keep running.

Now she knew where the smell of charring meat had come from. Someone had draped a human body over the top of the flame. Two legs, blackened but recognizable, dangled over the edge of the Torch of Science, near the ladder that an incredibly beautiful French youth had climbed back in April to light the flame.

Karin raced across the grass to the Torch, climbed the steps. She wrapped her arms around the legs and tried to pull the body out of the flames. When it began to come apart, her stomach churned, and she moaned. She backed down the stairs and stood on the grass, taking deep rasping breaths.

They didn't help. Each breath brought a great lungful of the no-longer-appetizing smell.

Karin looked at the ground, then at herself. She saw the greasy blackness clinging to her clothes and hands. She could feel it on her face. She suddenly realized what it was.

Only then did it occur to her to scream.

That was the first murder.

3

Professor Niccolo Benedetti showed the diplomat and the Frenchman his catlike smile.

"You have come to me too soon, gentlemen," he said softly.

Four men were sitting in the Professor's study, a dark, wood-paneled room on the third floor of Ron Gentry's house on the southern edge of Sparta, New York. The house had been a hunting lodge before the city had grown to meet it. Ron had gotten it cheap about the same time he'd gone into business for himself.

The Frenchman, a Paul Levesque, was controlling himself. "My dear Professor Benedetti! How can you say it is too soon? It has been three weeks." Levesque's English was flawless, if a little too precise. Much like Benedetti's own, Ron thought. The Frenchman was older than he looked, maybe ten years older than Ron. He was handsome in a dark, Louis Jordan-Alain Delon kind of way. He was here representing Baron Pierre Benac.

"It has been more than three weeks!" Levesque went on. He looked as though he wanted to loosen his collar. "Do you know who it is who has been killed?"

Benedetti nodded slowly. He seemed to do everything slowly. Ron had decided long ago that was in compensation for the speed of the old man's brain. Benedetti had been training Ron for years ("You are at least not *averse* to the notion of thinking," the Professor had said) but Gentry still sometimes had trouble keeping up.

Like now, for instance. Ron had known a half hour ago that the old man was going to send this Levesque packing, along with Pecson, the U.S. State Department man he'd brought with him. So why was he still stringing them along?

Ron suppressed a sigh. The only way to find out the answer was to wait and see. He settled back in his chair to watch the show. He wished he had a bag of popcorn.

"I make it a practice," Benedetti said, "to keep myself informed of the events of the world. The victim was Herr Professor Doctor Hans Goetz of Hamburg, a prominent astronomer."

"Prominent?" Levesque echoed. "Doctor Goetz was among astronomers what Niccolo Benedetti is among detectives!"

Oops, Ron thought. *That* was a mistake.

The Professor's chair creaked as he leaned forward across his desk. "I am not," he said distinctly, "a detective. I am a philosopher."

Mr. Pecson of the State Department, a little gray man in glasses, spoke for the first time since they'd all said hello. "I'm sure Monsieur Levesque meant no offense."

Benedetti ignored him. "I am," he said, "one of the few genuine philosophers left in the world. I do not devote a computer and the time of four graduate students to the enumeration of every possible use of the word 'but.' I, and a few others, concern ourselves with the basic issues of philosophy: What is real? How can we know? And what are we to do about it?"

"If I may say so," Pecson began, determined to say it whether he got permission or not, "with the number of your world-famous investigations—including the HOG murders right in this very city—a person might be forgiven for thinking—"

Benedetti smiled again. "Was I scolding? My apologies, Monsieur Levesque, Mr. Pecson. I did not mean to scold. I was attempting only to clarify. While it is true that my colleagues and I—" he gave Ron a quick bless-you-my-son look "—have occasionally helped bring evil men to justice, as far as I am concerned, it is simply a by-product of my true work."

The Professor's voice grew softer. "I study human evil, Monsieur Levesque. Where it comes from, what it does to the evildoer and to those who know him, and how it is to be resisted. I have studied this topic for more than half a century, and I am still not ready to publish my findings."

"But you do investigate crimes," Levesque insisted.

Benedetti shrugged inside his baggy tweed suit. "To study evil, you must confront evil men and women. Such do not line up at your desk to grant interviews. Sometimes, they must be sought. While I feel it proper, I seek them."

"I assure you, Professor, this is a proper occasion to use your genius."

"It may be so," Benedetti conceded. "But you have still come to me too soon."

Looking at Levesque, Ron could tell that the Frenchman had reached the point of wondering exactly how he'd gotten on this merry-go-round, and wanting desperately to think of a way off. Ron could sympathize; the Professor had often had that effect on him, too.

Levesque's eyes lit up. He'd thought of something.

"Let me ask you this, Professor. Do you not believe the Olympique Scientifique Internationale to be a good thing?"

"I believe anything that encourages men and women to use their brains constructively to be good."

"I shall not even insult you by asking you if you think murder is evil. In this case, we have not only a murder, but a murder, and an attack on *another* scientist—"

"You have not told me of this."

"It was a detail the police are saving. I understand they do that to screen false confessions. Does that knowledge make a difference?"

"It may."

"Then I am indeed sorry I didn't tell you sooner. In any event, these incidents are jeopardizing a project that I believe, and the baron believes, has been of great symbolic good to mankind, and may be a great deal more than that. Is that not evil? Does not every second that passes with the killer at large increase the harm done? How can you say we have come too soon?"

"Because of your attitude. You are too used to wielding the power of an enormously wealthy man. You have walked into the home of my friends and colleagues, in which I have the honor to be a guest, and you begin by telling me I *will* fly here, I *must* do this, it would be *best* if I said the other to the press.

"Monsieur Levesque, when I engage to seek out a *malefattore,* I do not accept what others tell me. I do not negotiate. I state my requirements, and if they are met, I then use the brain *il buon Iddio* has given me."

Ron could see Levesque relax. Just eat a little crow, or the French equivalent thereof, he had to be thinking, and this was in the bag.

"My apologies, Professor, I did not realize." The Frenchman gave the impression of bowing to the Professor without actually bending much more than a fraction of an inch. "I believe I can speak for the baron when I say you have simply to state your requirements, and they will be met."

It was a struggle, but Ron kept himself from grinning. Now, Benedetti would hit them up for his fee, and Levesque would come back with something about how can you put such a price on human life, and Benedetti would get huffy and—

"*Va bène.* I hope you can meet them. In this case, I will waive my usual fee."

Ron turned a startled exclamation into a cough. This was unprecedented. Ordinarily, Benedetti charged so much money it took whole towns to hire him. He told everyone it was a mark of the community's sincerity in asking his help, that the money itself didn't matter.

To be honest, Ron had to admit that that might even be the truth. Nobody, as far as Ron knew, had ever caught the Professor actually *spending* any money, but the old man didn't seem particularly excited about bringing it in, either. As long as he had food, shelter, books, paints, brushes, and canvas, he was happy. He never seemed to care much about what happened to the money once he got it. Ron's wife, Janet, in addition to being a psychologist and a former musical prodigy, was a whiz with figures. She handled the Professor's finances as well as hers and Ron's. As far as the old man knew, Janet could be robbing him blind—he never so much as asked to see a bank statement.

Still, in all the years Ron had known the old man, that huge fee had been sacrosanct. There were only two possibilities—Benedetti's mind was going, or he was up to something.

"I do this," Benedetti went on, "because I deduce from the presence of Mr. Pecson that my adopted country would like me to do this."

Pecson looked a little sheepish. "Baron Benac is a great friend of the United States," he said. "We owe him a favor or two."

Benedetti laughed. "Then I am drafted," he said. "After I fled Italy to avoid Mussolini's army all those years ago. *Va bène.*"

The Professor was serious again. "That will be fine for me—I would require only my expenses. But what of my colleagues?"

"Well, of course their expenses would be met, too."

"It is more than that. Mr. Gentry is a private investigator. He has his business in this city; he would have to leave it to accompany me. His wife, Dr. Higgins, has her practice and her classes at the university. I could not ask them to come without compensation, and I cannot function properly without them."

"The baron will make up for their loss of income. He is already doing so for the residents of Mont-St.-Denis. How much will be required?"

Benedetti proceeded to name a fee so high, Ron was almost embarrassed.

Levesque didn't bat an eyelash. "Of course," he said.

"Each," the Professor added.

Levesque simply nodded.

Ron shook his head in admiration, not even caring if Levesque or the diplomat saw him. So that's what the old sinner had been up to. He waives his own fee, to look like

Signor Generosità, then uses Ron and Janet as an excuse to bring a ton of money into the household. It would be a long time before the Professor had to worry about where the next tube of paint was coming from.

"You will find them worthy of their hire," the Professor said. "I trust and depend upon them without limit. But there is one more thing, and I fear it might be the most difficult condition of them all."

"What is that?"

"I require the full cooperation of the local authorities."

Pecson of the State Department cleared his throat. "Surely, Professor, you don't mean you wish to tell the police how to conduct their investigation," he said.

"No. But I do expect them not to interfere with *my* investigation. At times, I have worked closely with the authorities; other times, my work has paralleled theirs. But if I need a car, I expect a car. If I wish to question a witness or examine any evidence or visit a crime scene, I do not want the witness or the evidence or the scene to be inaccessible to me."

"Professor," Levesque began, "I assure you—"

"Forgive me, monsieur, but you cannot give me that assurance. For that, I must reach an understanding directly with the official in charge of the case. The Prefect of Police?"

Levesque nodded. "With the assistance of the Sûreté, of course."

"I must speak to both. The prefect, and the ranking Sûreté officer present."

"They will cooperate," Levesque said. "The baron owns the very land on which the town is built."

"But he does not own the Sûreté, I trust, or the prefect. I sincerely hope not, since men who can be owned are useless or worse. I will know more after I have spoken to them. Can you reach them by telephone?"

Levesque looked at his watch. "It is late afternoon in Mont-St.-Denis. I can try. May I use this telephone? I will use my credit card."

The Professor looked the question over to Ron, who said, "Go right ahead."

The Frenchman reached for the phone, but before he could pick it up, the door opened.

"Excuse me," Dr. Janet Higgins said. She was tall and thin and thought she was bony. Ron thought she was gorgeous, and had fallen in love with her the first time he'd ever seen her.

"Monsieur Levesque?" she said. "There's a phone call for you. A Monsieur Diderot."

Levesque grinned. "Fortune smiles on us, Professor. That is the Prefect of Police himself calling."

Ron picked up the phone, pushed the button for the right line, and handed the receiver to Levesque.

"Diderot!" he said, and went on talking.

Ron was rather stupidly peeved that he went on talking in French. Ron had taken French in high school, but its place in his brain had been taken over by the Italian the Professor had made him learn. He did recognize a phrase that meant "good news," but the rest was noise.

Levesque stopped talking and listened. The smile fell from his face like crumbling plaster from a wall. He said, *"Mort? Assassiné?"*

Everybody knew those two words.

Levesque handed the phone to the Professor. There was more French. The Professor nodded a few times, then hung up. He pursed his lips and put the tips of his fingers together.

"What is it, Maestro?" Ron asked.

"There has been another murder. The prefect found the body this morning."

"The prefect found it?"

"That is less remarkable than it seems, *amico*. The body was in his office. Captain de Blois of the Sûreté was sprawled across the prefect's desk with his throat torn out."

The Professor closed his eyes for a second, then nodded sharply, as though punctuating his decision. "Mr. Levesque," he said.

"What? Oh. Yes, Professor, forgive me. De Blois was my friend. We were at university together."

"My condolences. He shall be avenged. My colleagues and I will be there in twenty-four hours. I have already asked Monsieur Diderot to preserve the crime scene as much as decency permits."

Levesque took a deep breath and got himself together. "Excellent, Professor. I thank you on my own behalf as well as that of the baron."

"There is just one more condition."

"What is that?"

"When we bring this creature to heel, I must have one hour with him—or her—alone."

4

Etienne Diderot had joined the police of Mont-St.-Denis at the age of eighteen, as had his father before him. And like his father before him, in the fullness of time, he had become prefect.

He had been prefect for nine years now—he was forty-seven—and he was facing emotions he was too old to have to learn to deal with. It wasn't that he hated the murders. Every good cop hated crime. Every good citizen. And it wasn't just fear. If he hadn't felt some fear in the face of somebody who killed so brutally and disposed of the bodies so contemptuously, he would have scheduled himself for a mental examination. Fear was the proper reaction, considering the circumstances.

It wasn't even embarrassment, though the good God knew it was a humiliation for a policeman to find a colleague very messily dead and sprawled across his desk.

It was *resentment*. It wasn't supposed to be this way in a town like Mont-St.-Denis. Eighteen years as a policeman's son, twenty years on patrol, and nine as prefect had taught Etienne Diderot (or so he had believed) everything there was to know about crime in a resort town.

First of all, there were the small-scale swindles—shortchanging the tourists, or gouging them on prices. That was hardly a crime at all, and was treated that way. After all, the Germans and British and Americans and, recently, the Japanese only came to Mont-St.-Denis at all because they had money to spend on foolishness. The small-scale swindlers, working men in their way, were left alone unless they became so greedy as to become an embarrassment.

Next came the petty thieves, the pickpockets and room pilferers. These must be held in check, not too hard a task, since Diderot knew who they all were, and arrested them on sight. He kept them overnight in jail (subjecting them to a lye-soap-and-scrub-brush "prison prophylactic disinfection" in the process), then let them go, simply to arrest them again at next sighting. They soon moved on.

Next up the scale came the major swindlers, the smooth talkers who could flatter an aging widow out of her jewels or her inheritance; the young adventuresses who did the same to foolish men afraid of facing the fact that they were old. The prefecture, aided by Interpol, the Sûreté, and the police of the other Alpine resorts in Austria, Germany, Italy, and Switzerland, kept an up-to-date file on these. Not much could be done about them, except to warn the potential victim. This was a course, Diderot reflected sadly, that seldom worked, since the potential victims were working at least as hard as the swindlers to maintain the illusion of romance. For his part, the prefect was a realist—while the warnings might be useless to the victims, they at least ensured that the police could not be blamed.

Then there were the master thieves, the men who cracked hotel vaults, or snatched at gunpoint the jewels from the neck of a woman. These, paradoxically, were much the simplest to foil, for one simple reason. Everyone, on both sides of the law, was dedicated to keeping them out of Mont-St.-Denis. If more than one serious attempt at crime per decade were to be successful, the Germans and British and Americans and Japanese would go elsewhere to spend their money. There would be fewer pockets to pick and fewer lonely widows to swindle, as well as fewer people leaving their money in town for more legitimate reasons. Bad for everybody.

This was not to say there was never violence. Of course there was violence. Mont-St.-Denis was not a collection of picturesque buildings dropped near the top of a mountain in order to look quaint on a picture postcard, no matter how ardently the tourists longed to believe this. It was a true, functioning community, filled with human beings who came complete with a full set of passions and emotions, including the negative ones.

Some men beat their wives in Mont-St.-Denis, some youths stole motorbikes or smashed shop windows. But it was a small town. It was hard for a guilty one to hid among people who had all known him since he was a child.

The tourists, of course, did not all glow with the righteousness of saints, either. They got into fights with each other, stole from each other. Practically the entire incidence of rape in Mont was due to tourists too drunk or too stupid to understand what "no" meant. They did not get off lightly.

Diderot had, in fact, been looking forward to a year without ordinary tourists. Not only were these scientists respected people in their fields, they were here to work more than play. Diderot had expected a year of relative decorum, a sort of sabbatical from the more taxing of his prefect's duties.

But what did he get?

A nightmare! Two horrible murders, one in his very office, into which he did not dare now go. The kind of murders one expected in a big city, where the world had already gone mad.

Diderot was working in a small interrogation room. He didn't like it there. There was a one-way mirror in the wall that allowed what went on in this room to spied upon from the next. It made the prefect nervous, even though he himself had locked the next room and secured possession of the only key. He knew his nervousness wasn't rational, but he still couldn't make it go away.

Now Diderot happened to see his own face in the mirror. It wore an expression so sour, he had to laugh. Come now, he told himself. Think about the task at hand. Two saviors were on their way to help him—a new man from the Sûreté, and Professor Niccolo Benedetti, the wonder worker from Italy by way of America. Diderot planned to have a report ready for their briefing upon their arrival.

Carefully, Diderot set down all the facts he had managed to gather since the dawn Dr. Goetz had been found hugging the torch. He hoped they did this Benedetti more good than they had done him.

The customs man smiled graciously. *"Merci beaucoup,* Monsieur Gentry." He pronounced it "zhahn-TREE." "Here is your passport. It remains now only for you to hand me your gun."

"My what?" Ron asked.

"Your gun. Your pistol. Automatique." Still smiling, the customs man made a gun with thumb and forefinger, raised it to his eye and said, "Bang bang bang, no?"

"No," Ron said.

The customs man shrugged. "Pow pow, if you insist. But I am afraid *I* must insist on confiscating your weapon. The firearms laws of *la République du France* are strict in the extreme, monsieur. You shall be given a receipt, and may retrieve the gun when you leave the country."

"I don't have a gun," Ron said.

"Monsieur Gentry, I know you are here at the request of a man of high importance, but my duty remains, and I will do it. Please do not play with me the games."

Ron turned to the Professor for help—maybe this guy would make more sense in his native language with the old man translating—but Benedetti was busy charming the pants (maybe literally) off a dark-haired female customs guard. She was forty-six or forty-seven years old, the Professor's favorite target group, and she was blushing and smiling shyly as a teenager. Ron had to admit that the woman's face was lovely, and the uniform didn't hide a shape that was interesting, if a little too generous by current fashion.

Benedetti once told Ron, "It is one of the madnesses of the modern age that just at the age when a woman is truly a woman and no longer in any way a girl, she is often cast aside because of flaws that are merely cosmetic. This is as foolish as refusing to drink a vintage wine because there is some dust on the bottle."

Ron knew it was useless to try to distract the Professor when he was sniffing the cork, as it were, so he turned to his wife for help. Janet's eyes were squinched up behind her glasses. Ron recognized that sign. His beloved was finding his current difficulties absolutely hysterical. If she opened her mouth at all, it would be to laugh.

So he was on his own. He turned back to the customs guard.

"I'm not playing any games. I don't have a gun. I've never had a gun. I've never even *fired* a gun."

The customs guard made a sound something like *"pssssssh."* "Mon dieu," he said. "You are an American private *investigateur,* are you not?"

"Yes. It says so right on my passport."

"And you expect me to believe you do not carry a gun? Sam Spade? Phillipe Marlowe? Spen-sair? Whom do you think to kid, eh?"

Ron was just beginning to wish he *did* have a gun, so he could put a bullet between this guy's eyes and shut him up, when he saw an angry-looking Paul Levesque making his way through the crowd.

"Madame Gentry," he said. "Mr. Gentry. Professor Benedetti. What seems to be the trouble?"

The Professor smiled. "No trouble at all," he said. "I have been learning anew why Frenchmen are the envy of the world." The woman's blush deepened to crimson. Ron thought, why couldn't I have gotten in *her* line, instead of this addict of American mysteries? Not that Ron blamed him for that. Ron Gentry had been hooked on mysteries and detective stories since he'd first come across Dick Tracy in the Sunday comics. All he'd ever wanted to be was a policeman, but his genes let him down by giving him a pair of eyes so myopic he needed glasses to figure out which wall the eye chart was hung on.

He had decided on law as the next best thing. At least, that's what he'd told his parents. His real idea had been to get a job with a detective agency to help pay his way through school, then, by the time he was done, he'd have enough experience to qualify for a PI license of his own.

The plan lasted until senior year, when Professor Niccolo Benedetti had spent a semester teaching at Sparta University. Ron was walking down the hall, minding his own business, when a strong hand grabbed him by the arm, and a loud voice proclaimed, *"You!"*

"Me?" Ron said.

"You," the old man said. "You have the look."

Ron probably would have alerted campus security to a nut running around loose, if he hadn't recognized Benedetti as the man who consulted with governments and caught supposedly uncatchable criminals around the world. He was tall, almost as tall as Ron, and might have looked taller if his posture had been better. His body was massive, yet still angular, as though some modern sculptor had welded a few I-beams together at more or less random angles, then draped the whole thing with gray tweed. The head, above a spotted blue bow tie, looked small on top of that body. His gray-black hair was slicked back from a high, sloping forehead. He grinned like a cat. And his greenish eyes were eager to see anything the universe had to show.

Benedetti had been looking for a new "disciple." That was the precise word he used. From time to time, he would take a young man to assist him, and teach the young man what he'd learned over the years. Ron was the sixth and, Benedetti frequently said, the most remarkable.

"The sort of knowledge with which I deal is powerful, as are its temptations. Two of my previous students are millionaires, two are in jail, one is virtual dictator of a Caribbean island. You alone have taken my teaching and made it your servant instead of your master."

Ron wondered about that. If not for Benedetti's teaching, he would undoubtedly be back in Sparta, New York, serving subpoenas and looking for bail jumpers, instead of arguing with French customs agents about nonexistent guns.

"I'm the one with the problem," Ron said.

Levesque turned to the man in uniform. "What is the trouble?"

"I do not wish to offend you, Monsieur Levesque, or the baron, but the gentleman will not surrender his gun."

"I don't have a gun!"

Levesque showed Ron a palm and nodded reassuringly. "Have you not seen his papers?"

"His passport is in his hand. I have just returned it to him."

"What of the other papers?"

"Other papers?"

Ron reached into his pocket and produced an envelope. "I was just going to show him when he started asking for the gun. Which I don't have." He handed them over.

The customs agent read them, moving his lips.

Levesque didn't wait for him to finish. "All right, then? This man is ambassador extraordinary from the government of the United States. He could have a cannon concealed about him, and it would be out of your jurisdiction."

Diplomatic credentials. Something else the Professor had insisted on before taking the case. "If we do this at the government's behest," he'd told Pecson, "we must have government standing." At the time, Ron had thought the old man was simply giving the diplomat a hard time. Now he wondered if he'd seen this situation coming.

The customs man swallowed, folded up the credentials, and returned them to the envelope, which he passed back to Ron.

"My apologies, monsieur. Welcome to France. You may, of course, keep your gun."

Ron opened his mouth, then decided it wasn't worth it. He passed through the barrier. Levesque snapped his fingers, and two men stepped forward to collect luggage. They made their way through the airport to where transportation to Mont-St.-Denis awaited them.

5

The transportation turned out to be a helicopter. Janet Higgins Gentry didn't care for flying under the best of circumstances, and there was no way she could fit the idea of a helicopter into her conception of "the best of circumstances."

"I was expecting a limousine or something," Janet said.

"We're traveling three quarters the length of France," her husband told her.

"And driving is so slow in the mountains," Levesque added. "The baron is happy to find a use for his machine."

"Don't want to disappoint the baron," Ron said blandly. Janet looked at him, saw the twinkle in his eye, and realized he was paying her back for laughing at his difficulties in customs. She supposed she deserved it.

She squared up her shoulders, took a deep breath, and climbed aboard. It could have been worse. It could have been one of those bubble things with a little piece of oil-well stuck to the back. If she *had* to ride in a helicopter, it was just as well it turned out to be something like this. This thing, painted a pale blue with the word BENAC in gold below a gold fleur-de-lis on the door, was as big as four limousines. Inside, the blue and gold continued with a deep-pile light blue carpet on the floor, and a royal blue fabric on the wall. Shiny gold curtains shaded the windows. The chairs were blue leather with gold-finish metallic trim. Even the seat belts were blue with gold buckles.

Janet sat down and strapped herself in. She closed her eyes for a second, bracing herself.

"Would you care for a refreshment?" a voice said.

Janet opened her eyes to see young woman in a blue-and-gold uniform. She looked like somebody's executive secretary, and here she was taking drink orders. Janet declined with thanks, then watched as the attendant asked the men what they would have.

Ron asked where the helicopter had come from. Levesque explained that the baron had bought it from the French army, slightly damaged from the unpleasantness France had had with Libya in 1984.

"Fixed it up a little, I suppose," Ron said.

"Of course," Levesque said.

Ron nodded. "I hope so," he said, "because if this had been the way the French army rides into combat, I was going to join up."

Janet smiled. The thing she loved the most about her husband was that he could always make her smile.

She looked around at the helicopter again—she couldn't stop thinking of it as a mink-lined death trap—and reflected that she'd come a long way from Little Rock.

Janet frequently found herself analyzing herself. She couldn't decide whether it was a sign of vanity (was she so endlessly fascinating she could fill the hours in serene self-contemplation?) or a sign of insecurity (she'd better be interested in herself, because nobody else would be). The latter alternative was pre-Ron, of course. He had come along —handsome, blond, exciting—and shown instantly (to Janet, miraculously) that he was interested in her. He still

showed it, every day, and Janet felt lucky for it. She supposed that was a good way for a married woman to feel, as
long as she didn't feel she didn't deserve the luck—

And there she went again. Janet smiled. It was a habit,
that was all, an occupational hazard. She doubted anybody
would want to study the workings of other people's minds
if they found their own uninteresting.

The only thing Janet didn't allow herself to wonder
about was introspection itself. She had a vague fear that it
would be like wandering into an M.C. Escher engraving,
going down a never-ending staircase thinking about thinking about thinking about thinking. . . .

The stewardess came back to fill drink orders. Her
arrival startled Janet.

This is good, she thought. This is working. She'd almost forgotten she was dangling from an eggbeater God
knew how many miles over France.

More introspection seemed to be in order. Something
with a little body to it.

Like why it was she enjoyed crime work so much
more than anything else she'd ever done. She liked it more
than teaching, more than private practice, more even than
making beautiful music on the piano or flute or guitar.

Well, she knew why she liked it better than performing. She'd been *forced* to perform. She was a shy little girl,
always tall for her age, and gawky, with thick glasses and
braces on her teeth, and she hated the idea of being seen in
public. Her parents had assured her that she was a perfectly
fine-looking child, and besides, nobody cared about that—
they just wanted to hear the music. All of which was probably true. Still, as much as she loved music, Janet stopped
performing as soon as she could make it stick. She even
made it a point to go to college in the north. She'd figured

that since most of her concerts had been in the South and Southwest, she'd be much less likely to run into anyone who'd heard her play.

But what was the fascination that *crime* held for her? It was true that she liked to work with her husband, but that was only part of it. Janet had already become a consultant to the police back in Sparta before she'd ever met Ron.

There had been a time when she had tried to sell herself on the notion of being Useful to Society, but that wouldn't wash, either. The more Janet studied people, the more firmly she was convinced that there was no such thing as Society. There were just individuals making choices.

She decided it had to be an ego thing. Criminals, no matter how small-time, no matter how frequently they went to jail, were invincible egotists. There was the occasional Jean Valjean in real life, who stole because there was no other way to feed his family, but they were damned rare. Mostly, people stole and beat and killed out of an overweening sense that they had the right to whatever they wanted, to the gratification of every whim.

In idle moments, she thought of saying that to Benedetti, and ending his study into human evil right there. It probably wouldn't—the Professor probably had a dozen reasons why things were far more subtle.

That didn't matter. What it came down to was that these swine, too lazy or stupid or just plain mean to support themselves without victimizing others, were simply swimming in *self-confidence,* something Janet knew she lacked. Every time she helped the police or the Professor put one of them away, it seemed to even the balance a little. It helped her feel that the meek really might inherit the earth.

The earth, by now, had broken out in a bad case of Alps. Janet felt her shoulders pushed deep into the blue upholstery as the helicopter climbed higher and higher.

Something was niggling at her consciousness.

"Ron," she said. "The engine."

"What about it?"

"It sounds different. Faster. Higher-pitched."

"Uh-huh," her husband said. "Want me to tell you why?" Ever since the day he had spoiled her lunch for her by reading her a piece from *Discover* magazine that described microscopic insects that live in the eyelashes of apparently everyone on earth ("including us, I suppose") and survive by eating dead skin, "Want me to tell you?" had been a running joke between them.

"If it's because of insects, I want a divorce," she said.

"Thinner air in the mountains," Ron said. "The engine has to work that much harder to keep us the same distance above the ground."

"Wonderful," she said. "I'm so glad I asked."

Fortunately, she didn't have too much time to worry. In a couple of minutes, Levesque said, "We are here," and the helicopter dropped gently through the air, thin as it was, and put them down safely outside the baron's château. It had already been decided that they would dine with the baron later, but that now the Professor preferred to get immediately to work. Janet would have liked a nap and a little bit of bourbon, now that the helicopter had stopped moving, but the old man was the boss.

The doors of the machine swung open, and there, at last, was the limousine Janet had been expecting back in Paris. She didn't even get a chance to look over the baron's place—that was just a brick blur in the distance.

Now, like a good little elf, off to work she went.

6

Diderot looked at the faces of his audience to see if they still followed him. He had no complaints on that score. Gentry, the young American, was interested, but bland, like a man hearing a mildly diverting tale over a glass of wine at a bistro. The woman, Dr. Higgins, who Diderot estimated was one and three-quarters meters tall, most of which was shapely leg, and had to be one of the most spectacular women ever to pass through this place, wore a kind and encouraging expression, and nodded agreeably whenever Diderot made a point. Diderot understood she was the wife of this Gentry, but had not taken his name; who could understand Americans? He hoped Gentry knew he was a lucky man. Diderot himself recognized that his own good fortune in a wife had kept him out of many troubles over the years.

Captain Samuel Marx of the Sûreté, who had arrived just a few minutes before the Americans, was listening as though he were a worried student, and the final examination in this material would follow immediately. As in a sense, it would. Marx was the replacement for the late Captain de Blois. He was short and dark and thin. He needed a shave, and puffed away continuously on English Oval "A's." He was not only an Alsatian, but a Jew. Diderot had nothing against Jews; there were people in the town who were not so enlightened. He would have to make sure his temporary colleague suffered no embarrassment. Diderot suppressed a sigh. It wasn't the fact that the man was a Jew that bothered him, it was that he was an *Alsatian.* They had agreed to speak English, in deference to Benedetti's assistant, who was not sure of his French. Diderot was just as glad. It meant he wouldn't have to listen to Marx's *accent,* which had always struck the prefect as absolutely comical, even when saying things sour and sarcastic, as Marx so frequently did. The only thing worse would have been if he'd had to listen to a Belgian trying to speak French.

". . . So much then," Diderot said, "for the background. Now for the crimes themselves."

Diderot cleared his throat and opened the folder of notes he'd prepared. "Three weeks and six days ago, early in the morning of the second of June, Constable Ratelle, with whom you may talk if you wish . . . ?" He looked at Benedetti.

There had never been any doubt about Professor Niccolo Benedetti's listening as Diderot spoke. The old man watched with the air of a schoolmaster listening to a none-too-bright student reciting a familiar poem, expecting that the only surprises in store would be mistakes. It was unnerving.

"Later, perhaps," Benedetti said.

If Diderot had had any hopes of being able to step out of the spotlight, that ended them. So be it. If they thought him insane when he had said all he had to say, it couldn't be helped.

"As you wish, Professor," Diderot said. "Ratelle was on duty here at the prefecture when a man staggered through the doors."

Marx coughed into a nicotine-stained hand. "I thought it was a woman who found the body."

Diderot gave him a look. The prefect was beginning to think he had not sufficiently appreciated the late Captain de Blois. "We will get to her, Captain."

Marx shrugged, and lit another cigarette. "I'll wait," he said.

"The man who rushed in was bleeding from his left cheek, three scratches—no, deeper, how do you say it—three gouges. He said that he had been attacked from behind by some sort of madman, and was lucky to have escaped with his life. The man identified himself as Dr. Ion Romanescu, a Romanian national, an astronomer. One of the baron's guests. His papers bore him out, and of course, I have seen and spoken to the man since. Wait, I will show him to you."

Brilliant, Diderot thought, sprinting to the back of the room. I take the trouble to have the visual aids prepared, then I forget to use them. The prefect turned out the lights, then switched on a slide projector. The fan hummed softly in the background as the light threw Romanescu's picture on a pull-down screen that Diderot had forgotten was there.

Perhaps I am out of my depth, he thought.

He put the notion from his mind and collected himself while his audience had a chance to digest the picture.

"This photograph is from Romanescu's identification card," he said. The picture showed a man with a pale, unwrinkled face, wire-rimmed spectacles, and fine white hair that began at the crest of his head. He was unsmiling, and looked as if he were somehow in pain.

"Romanescu," Diderot said, "is seventy years old. He

has not left Romania since 1953, when he returned there after teaching two years at the Sorbonne."

"Excuse me," Benedetti said. "In what language did Dr. Romanescu converse with Constable Martin?"

"In English. As you may perhaps have noted, English has become a more or less official language of Mont-St.-Denis for the duration of OSI. Scientists, it seems, must speak or at least read English in order to peruse their journals, almost all of which are published in that language. As for my fellow citizens of the town—well, in any area whose economy depends on tourism, you will find most of the people can struggle along in English. Such is the power and popularity of Monsieur le Baron, that he has managed to persuade us to drop the cherished French pretense that this is not so."

"Bien dit, mon ami," Benedetti said. His French was better than Marx's. The words sounded as though they had come through a smile. "Please continue."

"It is particularly offensive to one," the prefect said, "that Dr. Romanescu should be attacked. One would think the poor soul had suffered enough."

"How do you mean?"

The voice was that of the exquisite Dr. Higgins. It came to Diderot with a sudden shock that to hear her voice in darkness was a remarkably agreeable experience.

He forced his thoughts back to business.

"Dr. Romanescu, I am told by those who understand such things, was, as a young man, one of the most promising astronomers in the world. He was, however, denounced to the authorities as a counterrevolutionary—by his own brother, a secret policeman. Apparently Romanescu's reputation in the scientific world saved him from a firing squad.

Romania, in those days and these, has never been a world power in science."

"A tennis player or gymnast they might have been able to do without," Gentry suggested.

"Precisely. In any case, Romanescu was kept under virtual house arrest until after the fall of dictator Nicolae Ceausescu in November of 1989. He has been proclaimed a national hero. All the other scientists, of whatever their political persuasion, have been saying over and over what an honor it is to meet the man. One said he hoped he would have as much courage in a similar situation."

Diderot changed the slide.

"And so, the man has endured years of privation, isolation, and perhaps torture—he is unwilling to speak of his treatment in detail—then, with his freedom still fresh, he comes to Mont-St.-Denis, where Etienne Diderot is in charge of public safety, and *this* is what happens to him."

Diderot changed slides. This photograph was in color, and had been taken under bright lights. It showed the same man in left profile. Three dark red scabs marred a pale pink cheek. Silvery whiskers dotted the face, since the scabs would have made it impossible to shave. The scabs were curved narrow triangles, one above the other, like pennants flying from the mast of a ship, with the pointed ends toward the ear, and the wider, blunt ends ending below the eye.

"Nasty," said Gentry.

"This was not the worst thing to have happened that night."

"Go on, please," Benedetti said.

"Romanescu described his assailant as tall, strong, and remarkably fleet of foot. He also moved in absolute silence.

Romanescu swears that he heard nothing until his assailant was upon him. He thought he was going to be killed, but for some reason, the attack was broken off. Romanescu was hurled to the pavement and the assailant sped away."

"Did you get a description?" Gentry asked.

Diderot shook his head, then realized that was useless when he was in a darkened room and behind everyone. "Not a good one. It was dark, and Romanescu saw the assailant only briefly and only from behind."

"Did he see anything at all?" Gentry asked.

"Just a few impressions. That the assailant perhaps had long brown hair. That he wore gloves."

"How do you give someone scratches like that while wearing gloves?" Dr. Higgins demanded.

"That is the dilemma, madame," Diderot said. "Romanescu's spectacles were knocked from his face when he fell. So the long brown hair could be a scarf, and the gloves could be mere shadows."

"That could be true," Gentry said, "but sometimes witnesses do recognize what they see. Other times they're making complete fantasies, and sometimes it's a combination."

Benedetti had been ignoring the byplay, sitting silently staring at the screen. If he hadn't taken an occasional puff on the foul-smelling cigar whose blue smoke danced in the beam of the projector, Diderot might have thought he was asleep.

Now, the Professor stirred himself and turned to his colleague. "Do you have a theory, *amico?*"

"Just a notion, *Maèstro.* Something that might be worth checking."

"Yes?"

"A black man. I don't suppose there are many people

of African descent in Romania; to a Romanian who's been attacked, shaken up, and stripped of his glasses, dark-skinned hands might suggest gloves."

"And the long, flowing hair?"

"Any number of things. A scarf. A wig, for disguise. Do you have any Sikh scientists here? They have dark skin, and they're not allowed to cut their hair."

"They're not allowed to commit murder, either," Gentry's wife said.

"Nobody is."

"Of course. My point is that if a Sikh is sufficiently twisted to attack someone unprovoked, he might be twisted enough to cut his hair so as not to be so easily recognized."

Gentry nodded. "Point taken. It's still something to check."

"It might be a woman," Marx said. "If a nongenius might be allowed to play. And the gloves might be gloves, after all, with clawlike attachments on them."

"Like Freddy Krueger," Gentry suggested.

"Who?"

"Nothing," Gentry said. "A character in a movie."

Marx scowled. "I have made," he declared, "a *serious* suggestion."

Diderot's head was beginning to swim with all these outrageous suggestions. Did Benedetti actually obtain results in the middle of such unrestrained fantasizing? Diderot's own fantasies on the topic were bad enough.

The prefect was glad, at least, to have the knowledge to stifle one of these flights of fancy.

"I think we may discount the idea of a glove weapon," Diderot said. "The medical experts who accompanied de Blois when he first came to Mont-St.-Denis examined Dr. Romanescu's wounds and concluded they were made by human fingernails, and rather short and blunt ones at that. I would think someone making a glove weapon would equip it with more efficient blades."

Diderot looked at silhouettes in the dark and waited for an argument. He got none. With a little grunt of satisfaction, he pushed the button to change the slide.

This was another identity-card picture. It showed a man about the same age as Romanescu, but similar to him in no other way. This man was plump and ruddy, and a broad smile crinkled his eyes and stretched a lusty moustache. The bald head had gleamed under the camera lights.

"Très bien," Diderot said. "I continue. This is Professor Hans Goetz, chosen by the ballot of his peers as leader of the optical astronomy section of OSI. It is he who has discovered the supernova in the distant galaxy. He was married and had three grown children. His wife, Gisele, which the Germans pronounce GEEZ-a-luh, poor woman, has promised to return to Mont-St.-Denis in order to be on hand should our investigation need her.

"She tells us that her husband was universally loved and respected, that he was so fair about sharing credit he sometimes embarrassed his colleagues, and that there was no one in the world who could conceivably wish him harm. Neither I nor de Blois, nor any of our men, in three weeks of investigation, were able to contradict a word the woman said."

It was true. Diderot had not been raised to love the Germans—no Frenchman ever had or ever would be—but the more people he questioned, the more he wished he had known Hans Goetz.

The prefect cleared his throat and went on.

"This was the man," he said, "whose burned and burning body was found draped across the baron's eternal flame later on during the morning of the second of June. He was found by this woman."

The slide projector clicked again, and the identification photo of Dr. Karin Tebner of the United States smiled apologetically down on them. Diderot announced her name and added, "She, too, is an astronomer."

Benedetti grunted, or perhaps mumbled to himself.

"Yes, Professor?" Diderot asked.

"Nothing. Please go on."

"Dr. Tebner is in the habit of running in the mornings. For her health. The habit is well established, as testified to by the clerk at her hotel, and several shopkeepers along the Boulevard de Ville, who see her frequently. The Place de Science, where the torch is erected, is along her normal route. It is logical that she should have been the one to find the body. Her screams brought the constable; she was in a state of near shock. When told at the hospital the identity of the man whose soot had soiled her body, she fainted dead away and had to be resuscitated."

Diderot worked his mouth. He hated the taste of what he was to say next, and wanted to spit it out as forcefully as possible.

"Nevertheless," he said, "Dr. Karin Tebner of the United States, solely by virtue of being at the scene of the crime, remains the closest thing we have to a suspect."

"After three weeks?"

Diderot switched off the slide projector and turned on the lights. He walked to the front of the room, nodding sadly.

"Things are worse than that," he said. "She is suspect in the matter of the murder only, not the attack on Romanescu."

"Not tall enough?" Gentry asked.

Diderot regarded the young American once again. There was more to him than met the eye. "Yes," the prefect said. "The curves of the marks on Romanescu's cheek do not necessarily indicate the assailant was taller than the Romanian, but the experts of the Sûreté have said that their curvature indicates someone much taller than Dr. Tebner, who is a woman of average height. That is, if Romanescu's story is to be believed, and I don't see why not.

"But even simpler than that, Dr. Karin Tebner had none of Romanescu's flesh beneath her fingernails, traces of which would have survived the most thorough washing, even if she'd had a chance to perform one."

"The experts have been most helpful," Benedetti said. "Were they able to ascertain the cause of death? I am assuming he was not held alive in the fire."

Diderot suppressed a shudder. To be burned alive must be the very worst way to die. Goetz at least had been spared that. As the prefect informed the Professor that the condition of the lungs indicated the victim had been either strangled or suffocated before being placed in the flame, he reflected that that was hardly a better fate. Strangled, then roasted like a *canard rouennais*. Humiliating.

The prefect went on to say that, assuming a constant heat for the eternal flame, they were able to be more accurate than usual regarding the time of death in the case of a burned body. In this instance, they estimated that Goetz had been put into the fire at approximately four A.M.

"Just about the same time Romanescu was attacked," Marx said.

"And long before Karin Tebner was seen leaving her hotel, isn't that right?"

Diderot smiled ruefully. "I have said she is our only suspect. I did not say she is a good one. It is theoretically possible for her to have gone down the back stairs and out the service entrance of her hotel, committed the murder— and only the murder, please remember—and to have stolen back to her room."

"But you don't believe it," Gentry said.

"Do you?" Diderot asked sharply.

The young American raised his hands in a gesture of surrender. "Hey, I just got here. At first blush, no, I don't."

Diderot grunted. "Neither do I," he said. "Nor did Captain de Blois."

"Which brings us," Benedetti said, "to the captain's murder."

The prefect tightened his lips and nodded. "Yes," he said. "Yes. I will tell you all about it."

7

Ron Gentry was inclined to like Diderot.

For one thing, despite having to deal with the Beautiful People, or the jet set, or whatever they happened to be called at the moment, the guy was basically a small-town cop who'd been handed one of the nastier cases Ron had ever heard of, and he was handling himself with class. Too many guys in the situation Diderot found himself in would complain that this wasn't in their job description, and go back to handing out traffic tickets. An equal number would start to feel their badges weighing them down like manhole covers, and have sudden attacks of threatened machismo. They wouldn't work with anybody, they wouldn't take help from anybody. Most of the time, they wouldn't catch anybody, either.

Diderot stood up to the mess like a good cop. All of it, even the embarrassment of having a colleague murdered across his desk. He'd taken a while to chew it before he'd managed to spit it out, but it had come, solid, professional, and unemotional. Diderot was a good cop and a smart cop, smart enough to know where he lacked expertise.

The other reason Ron liked him was that the prefect was so obviously smitten with Janet.

Ron divided the men in the world into two classes: 1)

Those who could appreciate his wife's unique beauty, brains, and charm, and 2) jerks. It was Ron's good fortune that Janet had apparently endured a continual parade of jerks until he had come along, but it had given her an insecurity and a shyness that she'd never been able to shake. Ron was no psychologist, but it stood to reason that being sincerely admired had to be good for your ego. So he was happy whenever he and Janet ran across someone like Diderot.

He'd already had it out with himself about the possibility that one of these class 1 types might admire his wife so much he'd try to do something about it. He wasn't worried; Janet wouldn't be interested. Ron had no trouble with his own ego.

Diderot took a deep breath and began by telling of his working arrangements with Captain de Blois. Diderot had concentrated on interrogating the townspeople, the man from the Sûreté on the scientists. After preliminary investigations, they compared notes, then switched for the next round of talks. Finally, they had pursued everything promising together.

"This," the prefect said, "was not a long process, since there was so little promising. There was the possible motive of professional jealousy, since Dr. Goetz was the one who discovered this exploding star, and we pressed all the astronomers diligently on that topic. As I have said, however, there was nothing."

Diderot sighed. "It was I, perhaps, who was the catalyst for de Blois's murder."

"How could that be?" Janet asked.

"Since the probable did not yield anything, de Blois and I got together to imagine the improbable. I suggested that despite precautions, perhaps someone here might be an impostor, perhaps a criminal on the run or an international terrorist, who had murdered one of the scientists and taken his place. Or hers. Perhaps Goetz had recognized someone as an impostor, and was killed before he could make his suspicions known."

"That does not account," Benedetti said with the irksome good nature Ron had never been able to break him of, "for the attack on Dr. Romanescu."

Diderot looked at the Professor for a long moment with his lips tight. "No," he said sharply. "It does not. But it was something else to do, rather than to wait in the office until the murderer's conscience brought him to us, *hein?*"

"Quite so," Benedetti said. The old man was completely unaware of the reason for Diderot's sudden bad temper. For someone newspapers and magazines around the world routinely called "a true genius" and "one of the world's great brains," Benedetti could be amazingly dense at times.

"De Blois handled the details," the prefect continued. "He got in contact with the governments of all the nations represented by the scientists, and asked for copies of their fingerprints from their identity registration. This was a simple matter, except in the case of the United States—" Diderot looked balefully at Ron, as though blaming him, personally, "—which apparently has so little regard for the safety of its citizens that it keeps no identity files on the general populace whatever. No wonder you must all go about with revolvers on your hips."

Ron was a hero. He kept his mouth shut.

"But that is beside the point. Since the Americans had all worked on a government project, or under government financing at one point or another, we were able to obtain fingerprints at last for the American scientists.

"The next step was to obtain the fingerprints of the scientists themselves. To do this, we had to overcome the objections of the baron. Have you met the baron?"

"Not yet," Ron said.

Diderot grunted. "The baron was afraid his guests might be offended. Only by continual repetition did it become apparent to him that his guests, if they were reasonable human beings, would find the murder of one of their number and an attack on another to be more offensive than to have their fingers stained with ink.

"And so it proved to be. As soon as de Blois or I or one of our men explained the reason for the fingerprinting, they were more than happy to cooperate."

Ron couldn't resist. "Even the Americans?"

Diderot missed the sarcasm. "Even the Americans," he said. "One hundred percent compliance."

This, the prefect told them, had been completed three nights ago, on the first night of the full moon. At first, they were going to take the two sets of fingerprints—the international faxes and the prints taken in Mont-St.-Denis—and lock them in the prefect's safe. At the last minute, though, de Blois had decided he couldn't wait. He would stay in the prefect's office, if Diderot didn't mind, and go over the prints tonight.

Hearing this, Diderot said he too would stay, but de Blois wasn't having any of that. Not only was Diderot not an expert in fingerprints, he hadn't seen his wife in three days. Furthermore, Diderot was obviously the more fatigued, having borne the brunt of persuading the baron to let them at his guests.

"I did not argue with him," the prefect said. "De Blois was difficult to argue with in any case, and in this case, all his points were true. I made him promise to ring me if he found anything, left him the keys to my office, and went home to my wife."

"I slept very late the next morning, almost until nine o'clock. There had been no word from de Blois, so I assumed he had found nothing. When I arrived at the prefecture, I found the door to my office locked, as in fact it should have been. I opened it with my spare key and found . . . *this.*"

He pulled an eight-by-ten photo out of a folder and handed it to Benedetti. He turned on the room lights. "I chose not to have a slide made of this one."

The Professor looked at the picture without expression, then handed it to Marx. The new Sûreté man regarded the picture with narrowed eyes before passing it along to Ron.

The photograph showed a man in a suit lying across the long dimension of a big, square, wooden desk like a sacrifice on an altar. His face was fully visible, turned toward the camera. The eyes were closed. The face might have been handsome, but it was hard to decide, because Ron's eyes kept going to the great red gash that took up the space where a throat should have been.

"Knocked him out first," Ron thought. Because of the eyes, and because of the way the blood was distributed in the room—it all flowed down the front of the desk, right from that throat wound. You could hardly get a tough cop, as de Blois had apparently been, to lie across a desk and let you rip out his throat.

"There was a blow on the back of his head," Diderot said, and for a second, Ron was afraid he'd spoken his thoughts aloud. "The experts say he was hit with a glass sphere I used as a paperweight, draped across the desk and then . . . killed."

"Any sign of a weapon?"

"None," Diderot said. "All the experts could tell me is that it was not a smooth blade."

Janet was looking at the picture now, trying not to gulp. Ron had coughed it right up when she'd stuck out her hand for it. It was useless to try to keep anything from her, anyway.

Now she looked up and said, "Even *I* can see that."

"There is still doubt as to what the actual weapon was —some of the experts suggested a loading hook. They were able to rule out the teeth of an animal only because of the lack of saliva in the wounds. Whatever the weapon was, it was something that pierced and then tore, rather than cut."

Benedetti frowned. "Was there not a constable on duty that night? How did de Blois come to be alone?"

Diderot shrugged. "There was a constable on duty, but he was out of the station responding to a burglar alarm from a jeweller's shop along the Boulevard de Ville. What the Americans call a 'smash and grab' job. In such a case, he is supposed to activate the device on our switchboard that rings through to my home before leaving the prefecture, but Captain de Blois told him not to, that he would cover any additional calls that came in. He said," Diderot added wearily, "that I needed my rest. The constable, by the way, is alibied by the jeweller, and by the contents of de Blois's stomach. The times don't match. In case you were wondering."

Ron had a couple of points he wanted to take up, but he saw the professor beginning to rub the end of his nose, a sure sign that he was getting antsy. Ron cut it down to one point.

"What about the fingerprints? Did the comparison ever get done?"

"It did indeed," the prefect said. "It was my strong suspicion that the captain might have been killed to prevent completion of the test. I did not trust myself; I did not even trust the constable who has been trained in such matters. I rang the Sûreté in Paris, and they sent me Reggiani. Captain Marx will tell you who he is, if you do not know."

Captain Marx, who reminded Ron of a French actor who'd seen one too many Humphrey Bogart movies, took the cigarette out of his mouth long enough to oblige.

"Reggiani," he said, "is the finest fingerprint man in Europe. A prima donna and a terrible, obnoxious man, but a genius at what he does."

"Reggiani," the prefect said, "was here long enough to perform the test and to anger everyone with whom he came in contact almost to the point of violence."

"And?" Ron said.

"They all matched. There was some of de Blois's blood on a few of the papers, but not enough to get in Reggiani's way. There are no imposters at the OSI, gentlemen, and lady."

"I don't suppose anything was missing, was it? The object of the attack might have been to take something away."

"Nothing is missing," Diderot said. "I checked and checked again. Of course, you are welcome to inspect the crime scene for yourselves."

Benedetti got to his feet. "Perhaps another time, Monsieur le Préfect. I congratulate you on doing a disagreeable job as well as a man could."

"A good man died because of my ridiculous theory," Diderot said.

Benedetti closed his eyes and shook his head. He put a

hand on the prefect's shoulder. "You are wrong, *amico mio,*" the old man said. "On both counts. Your theory was not ridiculous. And Captain de Blois did not die because of it. He died because someone has chosen to do evil, to kill. De Blois was fighting it the best way he could think of when he was taken. You must not blame yourself. Together, we must stop it from happening again, and bring the killer to justice. *Hai capito?*"

"I have understood," the prefect said, but Ron didn't think he looked any happier.

"Good, good," Benedetti said. "It has been a long and wearing day for all of us. I would like to see just one witness now, then repair to the château, sleep off this damnable jet lag, and start fresh tomorrow morning."

"Very well," the prefect said. "Whom would you like to see?"

"Dr. Romanescu," he said. "I would like to hear his fascinating story at first hand."

The second-shift clerk at the Hotel Etoile didn't look up from his magazine —the French equivalent of a supermarket tabloid—until the prefect cleared his throat.

"Monsieur le Préfect," the clerk said in some surprise. "How may I help you?"

"We wish to speak to Dr. Romanescu. I know the way —do not bother to ring his room."

"Monsieur, you have just missed him."

Diderot turned to Benedetti. The Professor said in French, "No matter, I will speak to him tomorrow."

Diderot was glad the world-famous Professor Benedetti was proving so undemanding. He turned to the clerk. "You will please tell him to ring me at the prefecture when he returns, to make an appointment to be questioned by Professor Benedetti."

The clerk's eyes and mouth turned to circles. "Professor *Benedetti?* The world's greatest detective?"

"I am not—"

"I have scrapbooks of all your cases! The Ghost of Capetown! The Sydney Bridge Ripper! The HOG Murders! All of them. I almost pity our local killer, with you after him."

"That is most gratifying, but—"

The young man's face fell. "That is why I am desolated I cannot be of service to you."

"What do you mean?" Diderot demanded.

"Dr. Romanescu has left. He checked out of the hotel, taking his bag with him. I personally arranged a car and driver for him to take him down the mountain."

Benedetti was grim. "How long ago was this?"

The clerk shrugged. "Perhaps twenty-five minutes."

Benedetti turned from the clerk, and it was as if the young man no longer existed. For the first time, Diderot felt the full force of the Professor's personality. It was like standing simultaneously in blazing sunlight and a howling wind.

"He must be found," Benedetti said. "He must be found and brought back here, immediately."

Etienne Diderot was out of the lobby and reaching for the door handle of his police car before it even occurred to him to ask what the urgency was.

Ron had been sufficiently exposed to the ways of Niccolo Benedetti to temper any awe he might feel for him, but when the old man gave an order in a certain tone of voice,

Ron didn't question, he just moved. When Diderot and Marx sprinted for the door, the Professor switched to English and said, "Go with them. Be prepared to report to me anything you hear and see."

Ron was glad to. He just wished he knew what was going on.

Ron caught up with the Frenchman just as Diderot was losing a fight about who should drive. Ron hopped into the back seat while Marx jumped in behind the wheel and the prefect huffed around to the passenger side. The doors were barely closed before the car rocketed off. Ron saw Diderot reach under the dash and turn on the siren, but by the end of the second block, Marx had them going so fast it was no longer audible inside the car.

By the time they left town and headed down the mountain road, Ron was beginning to wish Diderot had won the argument.

Captain Marx was a supremely confident driver. Either that, or he just didn't give a damn about dying in a flaming wreck. Ron could have sworn that at least half the time, the police car had one of its wheels dangling over the edge of the mountain. The realization that this was impossible was surprisingly little comfort.

Ron could see cords sticking out in the back of the prefect's neck. Captain Marx kept muttering what must have been Alsatian curses around his cigarette.

Finally, Marx said, "There they are." He took his right hand off the wheel to point.

"I see them," Ron said hastily. Actually, what he saw was a black Jaguar sedan with a driver in the front seat and a passenger in the back. With one more insane burst of speed, and one more flirtation with the empty space and gravity that waited off the side of the road, Marx passed the

Jaguar, then cut the wheels in toward the mountainside and blocked it off.

Brakes squealed. The cars stopped.

The three men sprang from the police car and sprinted back up the road to the Jaguar. This, Ron thought, is going to be very embarrassing if Romanescu isn't in that car.

The driver had his window down, and was filling the cool sunset air with curses. Ron didn't understand them, but he knew they were curses. Nothing else would have gone with the expression on the man's face.

A couple of badges shut the driver up. Diderot opened the back door.

Ron found himself looking into the frightened face of Dr. Ion Romanescu. There was a large white bandage on his left cheek.

"No," he said as the prefect pulled him from the Jaguar. "Please. Don't take me back there. Monsieur Diderot, please, let me go. Please. I must not be taken back."

He was speaking English. Ron was grateful for that much. "Why not?" he asked.

"Because it will happen again. Someone will die. Tonight the moon is full, and another person will die!"

8

The prefect tried to comfort him, but Etienne Diderot's
French seemed to have no effect at all—Romanescu never
even paused in his jabbering. Diderot switched to English,
since that was what the Romanian was babbling. "No one
will be hurt tonight," Diderot said. "I promise you." Even
as he said it, he knew he lacked the slightest justification for
making such a promise. Lies seemed so much more *naked*
when one made them in a foreign tongue.

Still, Diderot continued to make them. "And in any
event, I swear that *you* will not be in danger. If the Presi-
dent of the Republic should come here tonight, he would
not be better protected that you will be."

That, at least, was *not* a lie. Romanescu was the only
witness in the case; Diderot would rather eat nothing but
boiled cabbage for the rest of his life rather than lose the
man.

"You cannot protect me!" Romanescu screamed. "You
don't know what you are dealing with! Evening is coming,
and the dark, and with it, death!"

Diderot said, "Monsieur Professor, you are a man of
science. What can the moon and the dark have to do with
anything?"

The Romanian's eyes had been wild and unfocused.
Now they fixed the prefect with a wicked gleam for a scant

split second. Then Romanescu began to laugh in jagged hysterical shouts. He raised his hands to his face and sank to his knees.

Diderot was frankly at a loss. Marx, of the Sûreté, stood there like a window mannequin. Only the occasional glowing of the end of his cigarette when he inhaled showed he was alive. The man has seen too many Belmondo movies, the prefect reflected. The wailing laughter continued. Motorists on the mountain road slowed down as they passed to see what the fuss was about.

"May I try?" asked a voice in the prefect's ear.

Diderot looked up. It was Gentry, the American. Should he let him? Diderot knew that if this young man made a mess of things, Diderot himself would continue to carry the responsibility. On the other hand, things were well on their way to being a mess already.

"Go ahead," the prefect said.

Gentry nodded. "Thanks," he said. "This is the kind of thing Benedetti keeps me around for."

The young man walked up to the kneeling figure. Peeking between his fingers, Romanescu saw him coming and cowered. The young American squatted beside him. He began to talk earnestly, too low for Diderot to make out words. At one point, Romanescu's head shot back as if he'd been jolted by electricity. A few seconds later, the old man allowed Gentry to help him to his feet. The American put his arm around him, and began to lead him to the police car.

"Dr. Romanescu will come with us now," Gentry said.

Diderot felt like a man who had sneezed while the conjurer did his big trick. "Thank you," was all he could think of to say. Whether he was thanking Romanescu or Gentry, he wasn't sure.

Gentry got into the back seat with the Romanian. "Dr. Romanescu needs a place where he can rest and be cared for. Is there any place like that in Mont-St.-Denis?"

"We have a first-rate hospital, Monsieur Gentry," the prefect said. "In a ski resort, wealthy people frequently injure themselves."

Romanescu began to nod, like a judge weighing a well-made argument. "The hospital," he said, again in English. "Yes, the hospital will do nicely. Please take me there now, please."

Diderot's French soul provided him with several dozen pointed remarks he might have made to the effect that witnesses who make policemen risk their lives in mountain car chases, then dissolve into embarrassing hysterics, should refrain from treating the police as taxicab drivers. He was busily repressing these comments in the interests of his case when there was a rap at the window.

Diderot started, then turned to see the not-recently-shaven face of the driver who had been taking Romanescu away from Mont-St.-Denis.

The man wanted money. The agreed-on price for the trip to the airport was a hundred francs. Who was going to pay it?

"Who is going to pay it?" Diderot said. "Who is going to pay it? The fine for reckless driving is *a thousand francs*. To say nothing of fleeing from the police."

"How was I to know you were the police? The man told me bandits were chasing him. I was going to the police at Bernardine, down the mountain, with him. Was I to let my charge be captured by robbers without at least trying to escape?"

"How much does he want?" Gentry's voice again.

"A hundred francs," Diderot said. "It is ridiculous."

There was a rustle behind him. Diderot felt paper tickle his ear. He reached for it and found that Gentry was handing him money.

"Is that a hundred and fifty francs?" the American asked. "It's supposed to be a hundred and fifty. No offense, but your money here drives me nuts."

"It is not necessary—" the prefect began.

"It's desirable to get Dr. Romanescu somewhere safely while he's still calm, wouldn't you say? Besides, I'm on an expense account. The baron'll never miss it."

Pleased at last to have arrived at something everyone could agree on, Diderot shrugged, handed the money to the grateful driver, then told a softly growling Marx to drive them back up the mountain.

9

They were to dress for dinner; Ron was struggling with his tie; Janet had her own dressing room at the other end of the suite. There was a bedroom that looked like a set from a historical swashbuckler, an equally large sitting room, ditto, and a bathroom that (thank God) looked like the bathrooms Ron was used to—more or less. Everything that wasn't expensive wood was blue and gold.

"I knew they'd cut corners somewhere," Ron had told his wife after he'd been shown up to their room. Janet had been lying across the bed when he got there, having spent the hours he was tied up with the Flight of the Romanian getting over jet lag. Ron was still overstimulated and tense.

"What do you mean?" Janet asked lazily.

"Only one toilet. I mean, what if we both have to go at once?"

"If you stay in a place like this, you're supposed to be too refined to need to the use the toilet at the same time as anyone else. Can you believe this is somebody's house?"

"I know, and just one somebody, too. No baroness, no little baronettes. And this isn't even his main house."

Ron kicked off his shoes and lay down beside her on the bed.

"I could get used to this," Janet said.

"Well, don't. Private eyes don't make this much money. Benedetti doesn't even make this much money."

"Well, I'm going to enjoy it while I can. *If* I can, knowing I have a murderer to thank for the opportunity." She gave a little shudder.

Ron put his hand on her shoulder. "Shh. All the more reason to catch him, then. We can feel as if we've earned this."

"You're terrible," she said.

"Mmm," he said. "How much time do we have before dinner?"

"Not enough, damn it. I should be getting ready right now. I've never had a baron looking at my face before; I want to be extra careful with my makeup."

"That," he said, "is not the American Spirit."

"I suppose you'd like me to go in jeans and a T-shirt with no makeup, walk up to him, smack him on the back, and call him 'Pete.' "

"He would probably find it memorable."

"I would kill myself first, okay? And if you do anything like it, I'll kill you."

"You're beautiful when you're threatening violence."

"Come on, let's get dressed."

"Okay, who gets the toilet first?"

She grinned at him. "You go ahead, I'm too refined. By the way, did you see the bidet?"

"I saw it."

"Are you going to use it?"

"Nah," Ron said, "I'm going to stand on my head in the shower, the way I always do."

Janet hit him with a pillow, then they kissed, got up, and got ready for dinner.

Ron got his tie done just as Janet returned from the dressing room. "I need you to do my clasp," she said.

"You sure do," he told her. She was wearing her green silk gown. It was very demure in front, with a high neck and long sleeves, but it had no back at all. Janet had a beautiful back.

"You'll leave the baron speechless," he told her as he fastened the clasp at the back of her neck.

"Mmm," she said as she turned around and adjusted Ron's tie. Her eyes were owlish behind her glasses. Ron knew that look. She had latched onto something about the case. Ron had filled her in earlier. He'd yet to brief the Professor.

"What is it, dear?"

"What is what?"

"What is it that you're picking to pieces in your mind?"

"Why did Romanescu listen to *you?*"

"Thanks a lot."

"No, I mean why you as opposed to Diderot?"

"Maybe it was what I said."

"What did you say?"

"I said that he was coming back to town one way or another, and, while I didn't know what was troubling him, the harder he made things now, the more likely it was he'd wind up being shipped back to Romania in a straitjacket."

Janet shook his head. "If you were a psychologist, you'd be thrown out of about six professional associations for treating an hysterical patient that way."

"Well, it got his attention."

"Of course it did. The man comes from a country where until recently, 'mental hospital' was another term for political prison."

Ron winced. "Ooh, yeah. And he's already had his share of trouble with that system, hasn't he?"

"I think being denounced by your own brother fits the definition of 'his share of trouble,' " Janet agreed.

"Maybe I ought to apologize," Ron said.

"Just leave him alone for now. You've probably made him afraid of you." She smiled at Ron and straightened his tie. "Don't feel too much. It's better that he's back here, even if you scared him back, than it would be for him running across France in the middle of a psychosis. I just wish I knew what scared him in the first place."

"I think I know that already."

"How?"

"I was in the backseat of the police car with him heading up the mountain."

"What did he say?"

"It was Romanian," Ron said. "I think."

"Oh."

"However, I also think I know three words of Romanian; and I think he used two of them."

"I'm waiting."

Ron frowned. "Keep waiting a little, will you, honey? I'm going to feel foolish enough trying this out on Benedetti; let me tell you both at the same time."

"All right," Janet said. "But if you think you're going to sleep tonight before I hear about this Romanian you think you know, you're out of your mind."

Ron shrugged. "You're the psychologist." He kissed her. "Come on, let's go to dinner."

The sommelier came around (yet again), and Ron put his hand over his glass, and shook his head. He was tempted—

oh, was he tempted—to tell the guy, "I never drink . . . wine," but he realized that the urge itself was a sign that he'd probably already had too much. And salad, cheese, and dessert were yet to come, each, he supposed, with its own wine. Everything else had, except for the lemon sherbet that had shown up after the fish course.

He supposed it showed a lack of sophistication on his part, but Ron had never expected to see a meal like this outside of historical fiction. A succession of meats and fish and vegetable and fowl, each on a separate dish, each with a rich sauce. And each with a wine from the baron's own vineyards.

Pierre Benac could not eat like this every day, Ron reasoned, because if he did, he would weigh five hundred pounds. Not that he was anything like bony, but it would take a real stretch to have called him fat.

With his moustaches and imperial, his booming voice, and the pouter-pigeon attitudes he put his body through, it would have been easy to see the baron as a comic figure. But, Ron reflected, comic figures don't build—and hold onto—multibillion-dollar conglomerates. Or put together things like OSI.

Or, for that matter, play games with Benedetti on his home turf.

"But my dear Professor," the baron said. There were five of them at dinner—Benac; his assistant Levesque, the guy who'd come to the States yesterday (only yesterday?) to fetch them; and the Professor, Janet, and Ron. They were speaking English in deference to Ron (Janet's French was quite good) and that made him feel all the more provincial.

"But my dear Professor," the baron said again. "Surely it is a matter of definition."

Benedetti smiled a catlike smile. Ron could tell he was

finding this an unexpected pleasure. "So many things are," the Professor said.

"You maintain evil is always a matter of choice."

"Always," the Professor said.

"But cannot evil arise from *good* intent?"

Ron saw Paul Levesque, who'd been sort of moping along through the meal, hardly touching the food or the wine, brighten. "You must concede to the baron on this one, Professor."

Benedetti grinned. "Must I? Why, monsieur?"

"I have researched your investigations, before approaching you to assist us here. In the HOG case, the killer planned to *help* thousands of people. One can hardly think of a better intent."

Benedetti nodded. "Yes, and to fulfill that intention, this person committed cold-blooded murder and terrorized an entire city, causing the deaths of several innocent persons in the process. These actions were *chosen.*

"There is a difference between intention and action. Any rational being is responsible for the consequences of his actions, regardless of what the intended consequences were."

The baron stroked his beard.

"Very well," he said. "What of the actions of an irrational being?"

"I'm not sure what you mean. A tiger? A wolf? Obviously, since I maintain evil is a matter of choice, I absolve animals of it."

Benac smiled. "I believe you deliberately misunderstand me, Professor. I refer to an insane human being. Suppose the killer who terrorizes *this* town (and may God help us) is one of those dismal wretches who are driven to their crimes by madness."

Ron decided to join in. "Like Son of Sam in New York? Demon voices from the next-door neighbor's dog?"

"Precisely," the baron replied. He turned expectantly toward Benedetti.

The Professor took a sip of his wine. "One need not," he said, "let a demon persuade one to evil any more than the people of Germany needed to let Hitler persuade them. Or the people of Italy Mussolini."

"Just say, 'No,' " Janet said over a forkful of veal. Ron cracked up. He was glad that no one asked him to explain why.

"And a person who is truly mad—one who cannot comprehend the nature of reality, or the fact that his—or her—actions might even *have* consequences, is in reality no more responsible than an animal, and any damage done must be classed as misfortune rather than the result of evil."

"Then it does come down to a matter of definition." The baron frowned. "Crime or misfortune, the destruction of the Olympique Scientifique Internationale will be a catastrophe for the spirit of mankind! Mad or sane, you must stop this killer!"

Benedetti sat back with slitted eyes. "Oh, our killer is sane. That is, the man or woman in question has chosen to commit the evil that has been done."

"How do you know this?"

"It has been too well planned."

The baron was aghast. "Planned? A strangling in a public square followed by a cremation? A ripping out of the throat in a police station?" The baron stopped short. He shrugged. "But I am sorry. It is inexcusable to discuss such things over dinner."

Janet smiled at him. "We're used to it," she said.

The baron shook his head. "Well, I thank God I am not, dear lady." He turned to the Professor. "How is it you think such atrocities are well planned?"

Benedetti gave a shrug of his own. "Perhaps I should have said too well executed. Here are two murders committed in the most unfavorable circumstances imaginable, no? And yet we lack a single witness (except for Dr. Romanescu, with his 'man in brown' fleeing the scene) and not a single shred of useful evidence. It is possible, I suppose, that a murderer or even a madman could have such luck, but I don't believe it."

"Why not?" the baron asked.

"Ronald, tell the baron why not."

Thank you so much, Maestro, Ron thought. Recitation time for the man paying the bills.

"Please do tell me," Benac said.

"You stated the reason yourself just a few minutes ago, Baron." Ron said. "What is true of these murders that wouldn't be true if they happened right now in any other community in France? In the world?"

Benac frowned. "I—I am sorry, I still do not understand."

"Why are we here? More specifically, why is Niccolo Benedetti here?"

"Because I asked him to come. To find the killer."

Ron grinned. "We're getting there, Baron. Why did you ask him to come?"

"Because the gathering is threatened! These murders might destroy the Olympique Scientifique Internationale!"

"Bingo," Ron said.

"Bingo?"

Paul Levesque came to his employer's rescue. "It is an

American expression, *Monsieur le Baron*. It means you have won the game."

The baron's eyes and mouth opened wide. He turned to the Professor. "You mean to say that some madman is killing innocent people for the *deliberate purpose* of destroying this gathering?"

"It is a possibility that must not be ignored," Benedetti said.

"Mon dieu. Who would do such a thing? Why?"

"That is something we shall ask the killer when we find him."

The response didn't do much to cheer the baron up. To look at Benedetti, one would have thought he hadn't noticed, except Ron knew the old man noticed everything.

Now Benedetti turned to Ron and said, "But my young friend, you have had an eventful afternoon, have you not? You must tell me all about it."

"Here? Now?"

"Of course. We have no secrets from Monsieur le Baron or Monsieur Levesque."

"Okay," Ron said. He tried not to sound dubious. He'd known Benedetti a long time, and had yet to catch the Maestro not knowing what he was doing.

Ron reported the way the Professor had taught him all those years ago. First, a straightforward recounting of events, with all the dialogue, vocal tones, and facial expressions, then Ron's own thoughts, impressions, and deductions. In this instance, that part was taken care of simply by giving him an edited version of his earlier conversation with Janet.

"You know what Romanescu is afraid of?" Levesque demanded, when Ron had concluded. His handsome face seemed impressed. "I spoke on the telephone to Diderot earlier, and he said he knew nothing."

Ron shrugged. "He wasn't sitting in the back seat. Besides, I only said I think I know."

"I am amazed to learn you speak Romanian," the Professor said. "There are no ends to your talents, it seems."

"Very funny, Maestro," Ron said. "I said I think I know three words of Romanian."

"And how did you learn these?"

"I've read *Dracula* six times."

Benedetti was positively beaming. "Come to my quarters after dinner, *amico,* I wish to show you something. In the meantime, give us all a lesson in the Romanian language."

"Okay. The three words I know, if Bram Stoker got them right. The first is *wampyr,* the meaning of which is obvious, and which I *didn't* hear Romanescu say. I did hear him say *stregoica,* which means witch . . ."

"And the third?" the baron asked breathlessly.

"The third he said a lot. It was *vrolok.* You think of the strange figure with long hair running away; you think about this 'full moon' business, and it makes sense."

"I don't believe this," Janet said.

Ron ignored her. *"Vrolok,"* he said, "means werewolf."

10

The Professor rarely drew a cartoon before plunging in on a painting—he usually worked too rapidly—but this time he had.

"I was fatigued from jet lag," the old man explained, "and I knew there was little time before I would need to get ready for dinner, but I was drawn to the canvas." He pointed to the easel that was always the first of his belongings to be unpacked. "I simply took hold of a piece of charcoal and began sketching. I'm glad now I did."

Janet looked at the easel. The sketch was rough but perfectly recognizable—a hunched, hairy figure that was obviously a werewolf was running with an unconscious woman in his arms. A faceless horde of villagers with torches pursued him.

"Creepy," Ron said.

"The whole *idea* is creepy. Do you two mean to tell me you think there's a *werewolf* loose in the middle of twentieth-century France?"

"It's not the middle," Ron corrected, "it's more like the southern edge."

Janet looked at her husband. "Is that supposed to make a difference?" she demanded.

"You never know," he told her. "It pays to be accurate in this business."

Janet opened her mouth to go on, then saw the twinkle in Ron's eye. "You are very lucky," she said, "that I love you."

"Not a day goes by that I don't tell myself that very thing," Ron said.

"If I may interrupt this touching scene," the Professor said, "I think Janet has raised a most pertinent question. *Do we think there is an actual werewolf at large here?*"

"Of course we don't. I'm just reporting what I think Romanescu was afraid of."

"Why are we so sure he is wrong?" the Professor asked.

It was a new experience for Janet to see her husband at a loss for words. Ron was staring at Benedetti like a man who suspected the pope of using a joy buzzer.

"Because," Ron said. "It's legend. Superstition."

"Yet Ion Romanescu, a man of science, a man who has endured torture at the hands of one of history's nastier totalitarian regimes, ran screaming into the—not even into the night, into the afternoon sun—because he fears one is afoot."

"Well, Romania is where all that folklore comes from. . . ."

The Professor shook his head. *"Amico mio,* every culture on earth that knows the wolf has legends of the werewolf. All the others have tales of humans who become the fiercest beast they do know.

"It is true that in Eastern Europe these legends are especially vivid and strong, but has your devotion to Mr. Stoker's masterpiece led you to believe that all Romanians cross themselves and cower at the full moon? *Buon Iddìo,* you might as well believe all Italians cry *'Mamma mia!'* and slap themselves on the forehead when they are surprised."

"I'm sorry, Maestro," Ron said.

The Professor waved it off. "If the lesson is learned, that is all we need say about it."

It was a part of the relationship between the old man and Ron that Janet seldom saw. When Ron called Benedetti "Maestro," it wasn't badinage or a matter of form. He meant it—Master, Teacher.

"We still haven't answered the question," Janet said. "Do we give any credence to the idea of a real werewolf?"

Benedetti smiled. "I don't think we need raid the church and melt down candlesticks for silver bullets, just yet. On the other hand, what we *do* find may be something stranger and more frightening than any superstition."

"What do you mean, Maestro?"

"If I knew that, I would know everything."

"I'll tell you one thing," Ron said. "By tomorrow afternoon at the latest, this town is going to be *buzzing* with werewolf talk. Romanescu will bend the ears of the staff at the hospital, and judging from the looks on their faces, I don't think our dinner companions will be able to keep this to themselves, either."

"They *did* think you were nuts," Janet said.

" 'Nuts,' " Ron said. "That's why we keep you around, for these keen scientific psychological insights."

" 'Nuts,' " Janet replied, "is the word that says it best. All of a sudden they go too polite to ask any questions."

Benedetti showed them a palm. "I rather hope the town does begin to buzz, as you put it, with talk of a werewolf. The word, by the way, young friend, is *'loup-garou'* in French—listen for that among the mumblings you hear."

"Why, Maestro? Why set off a bombshell like that so early?"

Benedetti grinned knowingly. "Because we have been handed the fuse and the match. The full moon, the nature of the attacks. It is all too tempting to resist. Romanescu has seen it and reacted with panic. You have seen it, and reacted with skepticism. As the canvas shows, I, too, had already seen it."

"And reacted with what?" Janet asked.

"Humility," Benedetti said. "Always with true humility—a respect for the variety of the universe and a knowledge of my own limitations."

The old man took out one of his crooked cigars and lit it. "It will be instructive," he said, "to view the reactions of the others around us. One way to catch a pyromaniac is to study the crowd around the blaze for the smiling face."

"You have to let him set his fire before you do that," Ron said.

Benedetti took a puff, then took the cigar from his mouth. Smoke ran out through a frown. "This one is already lit," he said. "I am taking the admittedly risky step of fanning the flames to make more light to see by. I count on you both to help assure Niccolo Benedetti doesn't make a fool of himself."

"Yeah, right."

"I am not joking, *amico*," the old man said. He rose and walked to the window. He pulled the curtain aside. The moon was round and white over the Alps. "I no more believe in werewolves than you do," he said. "Nevertheless, I see the sky and am uneasy."

Karen Tebner tried to read. Couldn't. Tried to write a letter to her sister back in the States. Couldn't. Tried to watch

Knot's Landing dubbed in French on TV. Impossible. She didn't even like it in English.

She threw herself down on the bed, then got up and paced the room. She went to her window and looked out. She couldn't see the moon from where her room was in the building, but she could see the reflected glow of it from the snowcaps on the mountains in the distance. It was just too goddam picturesque for words.

What she wanted was to be back in the States, away from France, away from Mont-St.-Denis and all the sights and sounds that reminded her of early-morning horror and burning corpses of nice old men.

Of course, she didn't dare leave. She was their second most important witness. And since, if rumor could be believed (and it was Karin's experience that within the scientific community almost *any* rumor could be believed—all that training in accuracy paid off), the first most important witness had been hospitalized with a bad case of what Karin's Aunt Mim would call the heebie-jeebies.

Poor Dr. Romanescu. Karin supposed she was the only one at OSI who could even come close to imagining what was going through his brain. She felt shaky enough herself, and she had only seen the bloody aftermath of the first attack. Romanescu had actually felt his flesh being clawed. Karin shuddered.

She had managed to convince herself, during the month that followed the first murder, that she'd shaken it off, that it was a horrible experience that wouldn't affect her.

She'd stopped running early in the morning, though. Since that first attack she either ran at midday, dodging incredulous and irritated Frenchmen, or she worked out at the gym at le Coq d'Argent, one of the fancier resorts in town. As an OSI scientist, she had guest privileges, but she still felt out of place working the rowing machine in her baggy flannels. There had never, Karin was sure, been a more elegant place for people to sweat. It just wasn't *right* to exercise yourself to a frazzle, and wash it off by turning a solid silver handle in the shower.

But she'd done it. If she thought about it at all, she considered it a reasonable precaution.

The the second murder had come, the Sûreté man. That was like killing an FBI agent.

During the past month, Captain de Blois had questioned Karin probably nine or ten times. She'd grown to like him. He hadn't come on hard and skeptical, like the cops of fiction. He just kept trying to get to the truth. He showed her a picture of his family, a plump and pretty dark-haired wife and two robust little boys. He said he showed that photo to everyone he questioned, just to remind them that cops were human, too.

But since his murder yesterday she hadn't been thinking of de Blois as a husband or a father or even as a human being. She'd thought of him as the personified might and authority of the country she found herself living in.

And if this authority and might could get its throat torn out in the supposed sanctuary of police headquarters, then who was safe?

Especially the only currently functioning witness to the case.

Karin realized she had gotten worked up into a case of the shivers. She willed herself to stop. She had just about succeeded when there was a knock on her door.

Karin jumped so hard she was breathless. The knock came again.

"Mademoiselle Doctor Tebner?" A man's voice, low and slightly rough.

"Who's there?" Karin demanded.

"My name is Samuel Marx, Mademoiselle Doctor. I am a captain of the Sûreté. I have replaced Captain de Blois."

"I don't know you," she said. "Why didn't the desk clerk ring me on the house phone and announce you?"

The voice sounded amused. "Policemen discourage that practice. We are usually visiting less savory characters. The clerk is old, sly, and experienced. I did not request he refrain from ringing you, but I suppose he assumed that was what I wanted."

"What do you want?"

"To ask you some questions. I have only arrived today. Not, perhaps, with the fanfare of the great Professor Benedetti, but here to do my job just the same. It is time now for me to speak to you."

"Okay," Karin said. "But we're going to do this the New York way."

"The New York way?"

"I lived there for awhile. I take it you have credentials."

"Excellent ones."

"Good. Put them on the floor near the door, right near the crack." She waited a second. "Have you done it?"

"I am exercising great patience, Mademoiselle Doctor."

"Okay. Walk down the hall. The door is on a chain bolt. I'm going to examine the credentials. If you're anywhere near, I'll just slam the door until you come back with someone I do know."

"I had heard life in New York had deteriorated, but this is truly sad."

"Just do it," she said.

Karin listened for footsteps walking away. In the meantime, she grabbed the champagne bottle she'd been saving as a souvenir of the opening ceremonies. She held it like a club. It was thick, heavy glass. You could probably hammer a nail with it.

She opened the door a crack, saw a leather card case, snatched it, and pulled her hand inside. She relocked the door and had a look. Photo ID, papers, it all looked pretty official to her. Still, what did she know about French credentials?

"Is everything in order?" the voice asked from outside.

"Just wait a minute," Karin told him. She picked up the phone and called police headquarters. After a month of scheduling appointments for questioning there, she had the number memorized.

She was lucky enough to reach the prefect, Diderot, who had apparently stopped in at the station on his way home from the hospital.

The prefect wished her a pleasant evening and inquired after her health. She said she was fine, although she wouldn't have sworn to that under oath. She said that someone claiming to be a Captain Samuel Marx of the Sûreté was outside her door. He had credentials. She read him the identification number. Should she let him in?

"By all means," the prefect told her. "How long have you kept him waiting?"

"About ten minutes so far," Karin said.

She could have sworn Diderot chuckled at the other end. "Please, don't ring off until after you let him in. Just to make sure the man is as genuine as the credentials, I will speak to him myself to see if I recognize his voice."

"You're making fun of me," Karin said.

"I assure you, Dr. Tebner, I am not. There is nothing about this situation that is fun. If he does anything suspicious when you open the door, scream. I will hear and get you help."

Karin was less than reassured, but she went and opened the door.

The man who stood there was short and dark, ugly-handsome in a French movie-star kind of way. His suit was suitably rumpled and a cigarette dangled from his lip.

He showed her a crooked smile. "I would show you my credentials, but I no longer have them," he said.

"On the bed," Karin said. "Next to the phone. The prefect wants to talk to you."

"To me?" He shrugged, then walked over and picked up the phone. "No, no. I understand her, Diderot. It is your amusement I do not understand. Perhaps they will understand in Paris, when I make my report. Yes, I will confer with you in the morning."

Marx handed the phone back to Karin. Diderot vouched for her visitor, and that was that. It wasn't until she hung up the phone that she realized Marx had been talking English for her benefit.

"I'm sorry—" she began.

"Do not mention it, Mademoiselle Doctor. I am glad to see someone in this town taking this situation as seriously as it deserves to be taken."

"You don't think people are taking this seriously?"

Again, the shrug and half-smile. "I have been here only briefly, so perhaps I am wrong. Still, I get the idea that the locals believe it is something you scientists brought with you, and the scientists treat it as something designed to add spice to their stay."

Karin shuddered. "You can't be right."

Marx crushed out his cigarette in his fingers and looked around for an ashtray. Karin found him one, and asked him to sit down. He took a chair; Karin sat on the edge of the bed.

"Time will tell, mademoiselle. You may judge for yourself, of course. Just keep what I have said in mind as you mingle with your colleagues."

Marx lit a new cigarette. "And that, Mademoiselle Doctor, is why I am here."

"Try calling me Karin," she suggested. "Mademoiselle Doctor is too much of a mouthful."

That earned her a whole smile. *"Très bien.* Karin it shall be. I have come, Karin, to ask you to accompany me to the observatory. I wish to talk to your colleagues, to see the place where Dr. Goetz has done his work. To get, how is it said, a *feel* for the situation. I have much catching up to do."

"No one is there tonight," Karin pointed out. "Not in our section."

"I understand. But had Goetz no interaction with those in other sections?"

"Oh, of course. Just to drink coffee together, if nothing else."

"Then I wish to speak to them. Your presence will help me."

"I don't see how."

"I have been given to understand that with Dr. Goetz dead and Dr. Romanescu hospitalized and incoherent—and believe me, as one who has just come from several hours of trying to talk to him, he *is* incoherent—then *you* are senior member of your section, and will direct the study of this special star of yours."

"My God," Karin said.

"Is something wrong?"

"No," Karin said. *Yes,* she thought. Plenty was wrong. She was amazed at herself for not having realized that she'd be in charge now. Not that there was much of a section left to run—just her, a promising young Zimbabwean named Boza, and a couple of technicians. She was also appalled at herself for the unkillable tickle of delight that ran through her at the knowledge that the OSI study of the supernova would be directed by her. And she was afraid of what Marx and his colleagues might be implying from the fact. Had anyone ever committed murder over something that happened millions of years ago in another galaxy?

"Of course," Marx was saying when she tuned back in, "if you already have plans for the evening . . ."

"No, no. I was just . . . hanging out."

Again the crooked smile. "I am a poor excuse for a Frenchman, no? I find a lovely woman alone on a beautiful moonlit evening, and what do I do? I take her to work. My apologies."

Karin smiled in spite of herself. She knew she was being manipulated, that he was *trying* to put her at ease, but she didn't mind. She was glad he was making the effort.

"Just let me get my jacket," she said.

Marx drove a small Citroën, a totally middle-class car. It surprised her. She had expected a movie-starrish sports car with a canvas snap-up roof. He drove her across town to the base of the cable car that would take them up the mountain to the observatory.

Marx knocked on the door of the attendant's shed. They waited a long minute before a blowsy middle-aged woman came out grumbling something about why couldn't people wait until the end of *Knot's Landing*. That's what Marx told Karin she said, anyway.

Karin and the Sûreté man climbed aboard a red-and-white cable car about half the size of a school bus. They had the place to themselves.

"Better sit down," Karin said.

Marx shrugged and sat. There was a scraping, then a jolt, and the front of the cable car swung upward. Marx started, grabbing his seat.

"Does that every time," Karin explained. "Scares me to death. I should have warned you. I wonder why someone who hates these things as much as I do picked a job that always takes me to the tops of mountains."

"When you face your fear, you defeat it," Marx said.

"Defeat it, maybe, but it keeps coming back for more."

"Tell me about Herr Professor Doctor Hans Goetz," Marx said.

It took about twenty minutes for the cable car to reach the observatory. Karin spent the first half of it talking about Goetz and the rest of her colleagues.

"There was no jealousy? No animosity?"

Karin shook her head. "In our section, we all loved him. The three of us. He was a legend, but he was so kind. He helped me a lot; he went out of his way to ease Dr. Romanescu back into harness—the poor man had been away so long. He told Dr. Boza he'd wind up being the first great African astronomer since the ancient days."

"Yet he was the one whose name will be permanently written in the sky. No jealousy there?"

"Oh," Karin said. "Well, maybe. Of course, I'd like to have my name written in the sky. I like that phrase, by the way."

"Thank you."

"But it's already *there*. Once Dr. Goetz reported his sighting, it was *his,* you see. Nobody could do anything to change it. And anyway, what about the attack on Dr. Romanescu? Or the murder of Captain de Blois?"

"I do not know what about them. I can only proceed as I have been taught to proceed. There is no need to be defensive. Now what about the other sections, practicing other forms of astronomy?"

"No jealousy. They think we eyeball astronomers are rather quaint. Ted Llewellyn—he's a Welsh radioastronomer—calls us 'Thomases.' "

"Thomases?"

"We won't believe unless we see."

Suddenly, the car cleared the shadow of the next mountain, and there was the moon, looming over the valleys of the French Alps. It looked enormous, like a silver balloon Karin could catch, if she'd just lower the window.

Just looking at it, she went cold. Captain Marx, too, seemed to be looking at her coldly, and he too had fallen silent.

Images flashed across Karin's mind. Hands on her throat. The door of the cable car slid open, her unconscious body thrown to the rocks below. A trip back for the man with the cigarette in his mouth, and an attack on the fat woman who ran the cable car. And she could be gone and no one would know, not even the desk clerk at the hotel, because they'd left down the back stairs to have a shorter walk to Marx's car.

A policeman, Karin thought. A policeman had the best chance to be the killer and get away with it. And she'd be dead and broken on the rocks below—

"It's beautiful, isn't it?" Marx said gently, and Karin nearly jumped out of her skin.

"What is?"

"The moon. So lovely. How typical of people, to think such a beautiful thing could have evil power."

"I—I've never thought about it."

Again, the shrug. "Ah, well, it is not good for a policeman to be too philosophical, eh? But here we are. Does this thing behave as obnoxiously arriving as it does departing?" He suddenly looked concerned. "Mademois—I mean Karin. Is everything all right? You look ill."

As the cable car ground to a stop, Karin cursed herself for a hyperimaginative idiot. "No, I'm fine," she said. She gave Marx a mental apology.

The visit to the observatory was anticlimactic, after her vaporings on the way up. She introduced Marx around, then sat in Dr. Goetz's office—soon to be hers, she supposed—and worked up a schedule for herself and Boza, and the others.

On the way back down the mountain, Marx asked her if she would care to join him in a glass of wine. Karin was tired, but she figured she owed it to him to accept. He took her to a dark little bistro, where a piano player sang sad songs in that quavery way French singers have. They talked about things that had nothing to do with crime. Karin looked in Marx's sad, dark eyes, always behind their curtain of cigarette smoke, and wondered about the power of the moon.

11

Levesque rose early and went to the office wing of the château. He walked into the fax room, to the machine with the extra wide carriage, and took a look at the headlines from around the world.

Since de Blois's body had been discovered, Levesque had had the public relations staffs at each office of the baron's enterprises around the world on twenty-four-hour duty, with the most pressure, of course, falling on the people in Paris. That was where the media was. That was where the baron's major competition was.

Levesque knew that the baron's managing to make OSI a reality had been (in addition to the fulfillment of Baron Pierre Benac's sincere dream) a public relations coup of immense proportions. The fact that so many other giants of industry who might have helped had scoffed instead only increased the magnitude of the baron's apparent victory.

Now, however, with horror and fear loose in this place supposedly sacred to rationality and progress, the scoffers would be back. And now they could do the baron and his various enterprises real harm.

Especially Caderousse. When financial reporters in Paris (and sometimes even London, Bonn, or New York) were at a loss for something to write about, they could always try to determine whether Pierre Benac or Alexandre

Caderousse was the richest and most influential man in France. They never were able to determine which it was, but they invariably said it was fortunate that the two men hated each other with an intensity beyond reason, because if they ever decided to work together, they could control the entire country.

It was Paul Levesque's opinion that Alexandre Caderousse even now attempted to control the entire Republic of France; if anything happened to the baron, he could very likely succeed.

Levesque scanned the front pages of the major newspapers of France and of the world. The word "werewolf" turned up in a few headlines.

Levesque sighed. That much had been inevitable. Still, the PR staffs had done a good job on keeping the focus where Levesque wanted it—not that two grisly murders and an almost-third had taken place at Mont-St.-Denis, but that Monsieur le Baron Pierre Benac has brought in the world's most famous pursuer of evil (Levesque had given strict orders that the word "detective" in reference to Niccolo Benedetti was to be suppressed at all costs) to bring matters to rights.

Now, if only the world's most famous pursuer of evil could just *catch* something, Levesque would feel a lot better about things. Because until he did—or someone did—Caderousse would be sniffing around like a shark who's scented blood.

What Benedetti was to call the Folly of the Savants began about that same time. It began in the nuclear physics department. In a way, that made sense. For one thing, international cooperation on a face-to-face basis wasn't the novelty for these scientists that it was for some of the others—most of them worked full-time at the *Centre Européen du Recherche Nucléaire* in Switzerland. For another thing, they were here more or less for the honor of the thing. All they could do was analyze data. As rich as the baron was, even he couldn't afford to build a state-of-the-art particle accelerator, especially when the CERN machine, already the biggest in the world, was just a few hundred kilometers away in Switzerland, where the scientists could shuttle to if they needed to run an actual experiment.

But the third thing was probably decisive—the work wasn't going well. They fed their numbers into the computer, and the computer returned them nonsense.

"Merde," said Jacques Spaak. "I mean, shit." Jacky, as he liked to be called, was a Belgian, the son of a Flemish father and a Walloon mother, a combination only slightly less fraught with peril than the union of a Protestant and a Catholic in Ulster. He had assuaged a lonely childhood by immersing himself in science and in detective novels. Hardboiled American private eye novels with literary pretensions and titles like *The Rotating Chasm*. No little gray cells for him, despite a previous Belgian's praise for them. Jacky Spaak devoted his little gray cells to the numbers. In his dreams he was hard and shifty and could deal with babes and hoods and psychos without spilling a drop of his Code of Manly Ethics.

He turned to Peabody, an Englishman at the next console. "I am tired of this shit," he said. Jacky was glad that English had become the more or less official language of OSI, because even though he was a native speaker of French, Frenchmen found his Belgian accent nothing short of hilarious. It did not sit well with him. Nobody laughed at Humphrey Bogart's lisp.

Peabody looked like the international caricature of a scientist. He was thin and balding, had an air of distraction, and wore both braces and a belt.

Without looking up from his monitor, he said, "Which shit is that, old boy?"

"The numbers. If there is a graviton in this experiment, I am not going to find it today."

"Excellent," Peabody said. "I shan't have to share the Nobel, then."

"How can they expect us to concentrate when there is a mad-dog killer stalking us?"

Peabody's eyes were still riveted to the screen. "We're scientists, old boy. We're supposed to concentrate. Just as I can still concentrate on these data with you filling the air with nonsense."

"It is not nonsense," Jacky insisted. "What are you calling nonsense?"

Peabody looked up from his console and pushed his half-glasses up his thin nose. "The idea that a killer is stalking us. And what kind of 'us' did you have in mind, anyway? You and me? The nuclear physics unit?"

"Stop playing the fool. By 'us,' I mean the people at OSI."

"Jacky, dear boy, there have been two murders. One of a scientist, and one of a policeman. No statistically valid influence can be drawn from that whatsoever. If there were to be a next victim, and it turned out to be a barmaid from one of the resorts, you'd look like a bloody fool with your theory about some madman stalking us, wouldn't you?"

It wasn't supposed to go like this. *Jacky* was supposed to be the cool one, the one with the observation, analysis, and conversational skills to back the person foolish enough to argue with him into a corner. That was how it always worked for Spenser.

Instead, he found himself mentally grasping at straws.

"Perhaps, but what about Dr. Romanescu?"

"What about him?"

"He was a scientist; he was also attacked—the fact that he is alive is a matter of purest luck. And I have heard the fear of what he has seen has driven him insane."

"Eyeball astronomers are all insane," Peabody observed. "To actually *volunteer* to work those ridiculous hours. But fine, he was attacked. So what?"

"All of a sudden it's two out of three, my friend Peabody. Sixty-six point six repeating percent."

"The sample is still vanishingly small, old boy."

Jacky shook his head, half in disbelief, half in disgust. "I don't understand you. Even if this madman isn't singling out scientists, are you not shaking in the shoes anyway that he is at large in this town?"

"Your shoes," Peabody said.

"What?"

"The idiom is shaking in *your* shoes, not *the* shoes. At least that's the way they'd put it in those vile American shockers you've always got peeking out of your pocket. The correct *English* for the thing would be 'shaking in your *boots.'* "

"Well, aren't you?"

"Shaking? Dear Lord, no, Cambridge takes that right out of a boy, no matter how non-U he starts out."

"Afraid? Nervous? Apprehensive? I don't mind admitting that I, personally, am wetting the—my pants."

Peabody smiled at him. "Jacky, my boy, I admire you. You are perhaps the only truly honest Ph.D. in the world. I don't just mean about the science—I mean about faculty politics and publication credit and all the rest of the mess that goes along with being in the boffin business these days. Aren't you?"

"I don't have," Jacky said, "the slightest idea what you are talking about."

"I rest my case. Don't worry about it, old boy, it doesn't matter. I shall be honest with you in return. Of *course* I'm afraid. Perhaps not quite wetting the pants, but nervous and apprehensive, as you said. What can one do but trust the police? I can't see where it does any good to *dwell* on it."

"Not dwell," Jacky said. *"Concentrate."*

"Sorry, Jacky, now you've lost me."

"Concentrate on the problem. On the murders. You yourself have said it; we are scientists, that is what we are supposed to do. We have some of the greatest minds on earth here. Surely one of us, or all of us working together, can be of help."

"Let's not get carried away—"

Jacky's eyes were gleaming. "I shall call a meeting for tomorrow. I shall have flyers made up and spend the rest of the day hanging them up. We of OSI shall hold a meeting and discuss how we can solve this case!"

Peabody pursed his lips. "Do you think you're going to get anybody to come?"

Jacky wasn't listening. "I shall chair the meeting, and invite the police to explain the steps they are taking . . ."

12

They *all* came, all the scientists of OSI, everybody from every corner of the world, with their spouses, if they had them. They overflowed the original site of the meeting, the main conference hall, and still they came. Paul Levesque, as if he didn't have enough to worry about, was pressed into service to find a new venue.

His first thought was the Stade de Glace, the local ice-skating rink (a gift to the town, needless to say, from Monsieur le Baron), but that was currently filled with the flower of Alpine French toddlerhood, taking their first uncertain glides on the ice. Even if Levesque were to have been so foolish as to chase the little angels away from their fun, there was the matter of the ice, which could not be removed in less than twenty-four hours. So much for that.

He thought of Champs Benac, the local soccer stadium, which could certainly hold the eager scientists (it could hold the entire town) but decided against it when the radio told him it looked like rain.

Finally, a harried series of phone calls to the local monsignor and the bishop of the diocese had secured permission to use the Cathedral of St.-Denis, which was *not* a gift from Monsieur le Baron, but a great pile of graven stone erected over the course of the sixteenth century by generations of the shepherds and cheesemakers who used to populate these mountains before the discovery of downhill skiing. They had voluntarily taxed themselves and labored to build the thing, for no other reason than the greater glory of God.

Looking at it now, seeing angels and gargoyles looking back at him, Levesque wondered if, in spite of all the baron's efforts, mankind was not sometimes backing up as much as moving forward.

Jacky Spaak gaveled the meeting to order just an hour and forty-five minutes late, which, Ron Gentry had learned, wasn't too bad for France, even when no change of venue was involved.

In keeping with established OSI practice, the Belgian spoke in English.

". . . Some of the greatest minds on Earth," he was saying. "For most of us, these minds are focused on the future, for in the future, we can hope all the problems of the present will be solved.

"But now, the present demands our attention. The here and now. Somewhere in this town is a dangerous killer—"

There was a mumble from the assembled scientists.

"—who strikes brutally and without warning. One of our number has been killed, and another, who has already gone through too much, barely escaped with his life.

"Your presence here today shows that you agree that we owe it to ourselves and to our gracious hosts to help do something about this."

There were heads nodding in the crowd, approving murmurs.

"I am pleased to say," Spaak went on, "that the authorities welcome our assistance!"

Applause.

Ron looked around the front row, where he and the rest of the "authorities" had featured seats. He had to keep himself from laughing when he saw the sour looks on the faces of Marx and Diderot. When one of the constables had noticed one of Dr. Spaak's flyers stuck to a telephone pole last evening, he had torn it down and called the prefect. Diderot had been all set to ban the meeting. Fortunately, Ron and Janet had been there picking up copies of documents and photos to be studied in luxury back at the château. Ron had (somehow) managed to get the prefect to hold off until the Professor could be fetched.

At the same time, Diderot sent for Captain Marx, and had him pulled right out under the umbrella of a café in a side street of the town, where he was sharing an aperitif with Dr. Tebner, the American astronomer. Ron had noticed no great love between Marx and Diderot, but Marx was unstinting in his moral support of the prefect during the conversation that ensued.

"The whole idea is nauseating," Marx said. "It is madness to let civilians meddle with a homicide investigation."

"Under ordinary circumstances, I would agree with you," Benedetti said.

"Ordinary circumstances!" Diderot didn't precisely tear his hair, but his voice indicated he wanted to. "This case is difficult enough without several hundred *geniuses, bon Dieu,* trampling over the landscape."

"How are you going to stop them?" Ron said. "House arrest? These aren't ordinary schmoes, you know—"

Marx frowned darkly. "Schmoes? What does this mean, this 'schmoes'?"

"People of no special significance," Ron explained. A stray French phrase sprang to mind. "Like 'Jacques Bonhomme,' only less respectful."

Marx nodded. "I see. Schmoes."

"Yeah. That's what we're *not* dealing with here," Ron said. "These people are world-famous in their fields, and they are the honored guests of the baron, the Republic of France, and the town of Mont-St.-Denis."

"God help me," Diderot said ruefully while crossing himself. "Then what am I to do? I certainly cannot allow these people to come in and out of my office like what do you call it—Jacks-in-the-boxes. Can we find no way to dampen this enthusiasm?"

"It's not enthusiasm," Janet said. "It's fear."

Diderot looked at her. "It pains me to differ with you, dear lady, but what I see is a horde of desk-bound pencil-pushers grabbing at something they would like to think of as a great adventure. Sherlock Holmes with his game afoot or some similar nonsense."

Janet shook her head. "No," she said. "Oh, there's some of that, but it's a mask for what's really going on."

"Please then, tell us what is really going on." There was a frank sneer on Captain Marx's face when he said it.

"These people live in a different world from the rest of us," Janet began.

Diderot smiled in spite of himself. "That, madame, we have already been able to discover for ourselves."

"It goes deeper than you might think. These are people whose deepest commitment is not to a cause or a country or even to another person. The scientists at OSI have made their commitment—and make no mistake, it is a deep, emotional bond—with their own ideas of reason, or maybe *rationality* is a better word.

"Their entire lives are devoted to making things make a special kind of sense—scientific sense. Some of them, especially those from more prosperous societies, may have turned to science because they were not very successful at making sense of the rest of the world.

"Then Dr. Goetz, a man at the top of his profession, a man who had just made an historic scientific discovery, whose success in his field each of them would like to duplicate in his or her own, is killed. Dr. Romanescu is savagely attacked.

"And no one knows why. No one knows by whom. It makes no *sense*. Not even to us, at least not yet, and we specialize in this sort of thing."

Diderot's grunt implied the French equivalent of "Leave me out of it, lady."

Janet went on. "They want some way to get control of this situation, or at least to tell themselves they've done so. They want to prove that with the exercise of the great skills they've developed, they can make this situation be rational. I think we ought to let them try."

For the first time since Ron met him, Captain Marx opened his sleepy eyes. "Do you actually think they can help?"

Janet used her eyes to shift the question to Benedetti. "One never knows," the old man said. He began to light a cigar. "I rather think not. When we finally clap our hands on the shoulder of this one, I believe he will prove to have been logical, but not rational."

"I'm afraid you must elaborate on that for a policeman, Professor," Marx said. His tone was neither as polite nor as patient as his words.

"Gladly," the old man said around puffs. "Logic is merely a method. If A, then B. Any premise will do as a start. The madder a criminal is, the more logical he is likely to be. If my mother has been replaced by an alien invader from Mars, then it is supremely logical to kill her with an ice pick.

"Reason, on the other hand, implies the attempt to use logic taking as one's premise the facts of the observable world."

"You think the killer is mad, then," Diderot said. "Earlier, you denied it."

"He is not mad," Benedetti snapped. "Despite the full moon and the savagery of the attacks, I am sure of it. Not mad, only logical. He is proceeding brilliantly after starting with the premise that epitomizes the choice of evil: that one human being may, for pleasure, profit, or convenience, dispose of the life or property of another."

"That is very profound, Professor," Marx said. "But I fail to understand why you think it wise to let the scientists have their Junior Detective Club meeting. Or do you? Now that I think of it, you haven't said."

"I do," Benedetti said. "My colleague will explain."

Once again, the old man had handed Ron a zinger. Ron had learned not to jump when Benedetti put him on the spot like that, but he was never going to learn to like it. These things were the pop quizzes that went along with being the student of Niccolo Benedetti.

Ron took a deep breath and ran with it. "Okay," he said. "First, if you don't let them have their meeting, they're going to resent it. Geniuses, as I have reason to know, have enormous egos."

Benedetti chuckled.

Ron continued, "If you don't accept what they insist is going to be their 'help,' they'll get in a snit; they'll say you're treating them like children."

"But they are acting like children!" Diderot protested.

"Of course they are. Unfortunately, you can't spank them and send them to bed without ruining the baron's whole party."

The Prefect of Police took a deep breath and drew himself up taller. "I should not like to do that," he said, "but if that is the difference between catching a murderer and letting him escape, I will do it all the same."

"We never thought anything different," Ron assured him. "But I think we can agree it hasn't come to that yet. So. If you tell them to go take a hike, they'll just go sneaking around doing detective work, God help us all, getting in the way and trampling on whatever leads may actually be out there."

"So what do you plan, then?" Marx asked.

"Bureaucratize them. They're used to that. They'll present papers detailing lines of investigation they think should be followed. They can work on these alone or in groups. Then everything has to come to the authorities— that's you, gentlemen—"

"Just a moment—" Diderot began.

"I do not have the time—" Marx sputtered.

Ron ignored them. "—by means of a review by Dr. Janet Higgins," Ron indicated his wife, "who is a college professor herself and has a high tolerance for academic bullshit. In any case, this will keep them happy and out of the way, and who knows? They may actually come up with something useful."

Diderot grumbled. "Organized that way, it might work."

"There's something else," Ron said.

"Yes?"

"Assuming our killer has access to this meeting, it's

going to be awfully tempting for him to show up. It's going to be awfully hard for him not to write a really clever paper to get himself inside the investigation. He can laugh all the harder at us, that way."

"It might be a good chance to catch him," Janet said, almost apologetically. "If I read the papers right."

And that had sold it. The meeting would be allowed to take place.

Benedetti gave them a couple of glowing paragraphs about how he drew energy from being surrounded by great minds, then introduced Janet, who gave them the procedure the authorities had agreed to. Ron looked at Dr. Jacky Spaak, who was beaming in his seat on the dais. On the killer-tries-to-worm-himself-inside theory, Dr. Spaak was suspect number one. A background check was already in the works. Ron reminded himself to have a few words with the fellow as soon as possible.

13

"I trust you will be more comfortable in the château," Paul Levesque said in English. It seemed he was talking English nonstop these days, if not to the detectives, then to people on OSI business. Now he was talking English to a Romanian who at one time lived in Paris. When this was all over (God alone knew when), Levesque promised himself a visit to his mother in Versailles, where he could spend a week or a month talking nothing but his native tongue.

"I'm sure I will be," Romanescu said tentatively. "I am —I am very grateful to the baron. I'm not sure how fitted I am for human company . . ."

"The amount of company you receive will be entirely up to you. You may have your meals in your room, if you so desire. You are, of course, free to come and go as you please. The baron simply felt that you might be more comfortable away from the hospital."

Levesque did not bother to add that the hospital staff was beside itself trying to deal with the deluge of calls from journalists and crime-crazed scientists, all trying to reach Romanescu to confirm or disprove some theory or other. It had been decided that it would be better for the man himself, the town, and what was left of OSI for Romanescu to stay with the baron.

The Romanian touched the bandage on his cheek.

"And yet," he said, "I think I would like to join the baron for dinner, if he will have me. I would like to speak to him, and to Professor Benedetti. I feel I owe them an . . . explanation, if not an apology."

"I am sure they don't feel that way," Levesque said. "They will simply be happy to find you have recovered so thoroughly from your trouble."

Romanescu showed a bandage-twisted grin. "The recovery doesn't go very deep. I still have nightmares. You must warn the staff at the château that I am likely to cry out in the night."

Levesque had interviewed the hospital's staff closely before actually going ahead and arranging for Romanescu to be released from the hospital. No one had mentioned cries in the night. It was good to be warned.

"I have nightmares, myself, sometimes, Doctor," Levesque said. "Everyone does."

"Not like mine."

There wasn't much that could be said to that. Levesque told the driver to pick up Romanescu's bag, and they went out to the car.

"I was afraid for a few moments," Jacky Spaak said, "that I had outsmarted myself."

Jacky's tone invited Ron Gentry to share in the amazement that something so absurd could even come close to happening.

"How do you mean?" Ron asked.

"Well, I was afraid that since the Task Force" (he had taken to calling it the Task Force) "was my idea, I would wind up coordinating it, spending all my time processing other ideas, then having no time to develop my own."

Ron shrugged. "I don't know. In my experience I've found that other people's theories have a way of sparking mine."

Dr. Spaak looked at the Real Live American Private Eye with something like hero worship. It made Ron feel stupid, and more than a little uncomfortable. It occurred to him he ought to introduce this guy to that customs guard at Orly.

"Yes," Jacky said. "Of course. Perhaps you and I could exchange ideas."

"Wouldn't be much of a trade," Ron said. "I don't have a glimmer."

"Oh," Jacky said. His face fell. You might have thought he was a kid who'd just seen Santa Claus pull the pillow out of his pants. "Well, I am still grateful to Dr. Higgins for taking from me the job of coordinating the Task Force. I would have done my best, of course, but I think I can be of better service working on my own."

One thing a private eye learns to do is lie, but what Ron had to do then was worse. He had to tell a truth he hated.

"I'd be glad," he said, "to hear your thoughts on the subject."

And for the next half hour he got them.

His wife, in the meantime, got *hours* of it.

Diderot had set her up in an office in the prefecture (not the one in which de Blois had been killed, for which Janet was more than grateful). No sooner had she settled into the hard wooden swivel chair than a line formed outside her office.

The first one through the door at ten o'clock had been

Professor Karagiorgiou, a marine biologist from Greece. From first to last, he grinned at her with huge, white teeth.

"Good morning, dear lady." He beamed. "I have come to save you time."

He was so cheerful, it was hard for Janet not to smile back at him. "That's always welcome."

"I feel the same way. I am not like other Greeks; you notice I am the first in the queue today, hah? I am not like other scientists, *pssh,* so naive." He slapped himself hard on a rounded stomach. "I am peasant stock, the son of sponge divers. They dove into the sea after sponges, I go after secrets of science, but the heart!" He slapped himself again. "The heart is the same! I am a man of action, a man of adventure, a man of the world!

"And that is why I tell you you will never solve this case."

Janet didn't quite know what to say.

"Never?" she asked meekly.

"Never!" Karagiorgiou insisted. "And I will tell you why. There is more going on here than just the two murders, dear lady."

"They were atrocious murders, Professor."

"Nothings! The tip of the icicle!" Karagiorgiou realized he was shouting, looked around slyly, then reduced his volume to a dull roar.

"Oh, yes, dear lady, to you and me, atrocious murders indeed. But to the people behind this, it is the snap of the fingers."

"Who *is* behind it, then?" Janet said. She knew it was ridiculous, but the man was so obviously bursting with certainty, she leaned forward in anticipation.

Still smiling, Karagiorgiou lowered his voice to a

rough whisper. "The Company," he said. He sat back, practically glowing with triumph.

"The Company?" Janet echoed.

"Yes. The Company. The spooks. The spies. The CIA."

"The CIA."

"Yes, and now that I have said so, I have no fear, even if you are one of them yourself, dear lady. They kill only for expediency, never for reasons a decent man can understand, like revenge."

"Why would the CIA want to kill an astronomer and a policeman?"

Karagiorgiou shrugged and made the *Pssh* noise again. "Who knows? They have one of their insane plans. They are distracting attention from something real. They are attracting attention *to* something real. I doubt if they know themselves. But can you answer me this: Why has there been no socialism in Greece after twelve years of socialist government? Do you think the CIA has nothing to do with that?"

It occurred to Janet that even without the CIA, it would hard to impose socialism on a people consisting solely of individuals who want to own their own restaurants, but she got no farther than opening her mouth when Karagiorgiou went on.

"And why is Karagiorgiou here, hah? A marine biologist brought to the mountains hundreds of miles from the sea, and told to work. It is ridiculous. I will tell you why. There is something at the bottom of the Aegean the CIA does not want Karagiorgiou to see! That is why they have held this ridiculous convention, to remove Karagiorgiou from the scene while they get rid of whatever it is."

He paused for breath. Janet took a look into the Greek's black eyes and saw sparks jumping, each spark caused, she was sure, by two or more conspiracy theories colliding in his brain.

"Thank you, Dr. Karagiorgiou. You've given us a lot to think about."

"Hah!" he said. He rose and kissed Janet's hand. "All the thinking you do will get you no further. Just take care not to cross the Company. Better yet, denounce them. Then you will be perfectly safe. I'm glad I have got you straightened out. We must talk again sometime." He sailed out.

Janet looked at her watch. Twenty minutes after ten. She was exhausted already.

"Next," she sighed.

14

Ron looked at the plate full of snails in front of him and felt his stomach try a back flip. He lifted his eyes from the table and looked around at his dinner companions, but that was worse. Everyone, even his wife (the traitor), was gaily using tongs and small forks to pull little gray blobs (with *antennae,* yet) from shells, and popping them merrily into their mouths. Several (including Benedetti) were nodding appreciatively, then wiping them around in garlic butter until they were shiny, and having another go.

What is the matter with these people? Ron thought. Haven't they ever seen snails? Don't they know that snails spend their lives sliding around in their own snot?

Apparently not. And he didn't want to offend the baron, either. Ron took a deep breath, seized the tongs and the oyster fork. Trying not to look, he plucked the grayness from the shell and brought it quickly to his mouth, thinking all the while, *"Shrimp scampi! Shrimp scampi!"*

It kind of almost worked. Ron chewed it a couple of times and got it down without actually feeling the slimy little antennae tickling his mouth. Now all he had to do was choke down five more. He tried thinking of the next one as an escargot rather than, say, slug-on-the-half-shell, but that didn't work as well as the shrimp scampi ploy.

What he needed was some conversation to take his mind off this, but the rest of these perverts had been too busy stuffing their faces with garden pests to say anything.

So Ron said something. "I'm sorry I set off the alarm last night, Baron."

Benac patted his lips with a snow white napkin, then used it to wave Ron's apology away. "It was nothing, the work of a moment to correct. And it keeps Hilaire from becoming bored."

It had kept Ron and Janet from becoming bored last night, too. It is far from boring for an armed man to come knocking on your door a few seconds after you open the window.

The baron had, at one time, kept a virtual army of security guards. "But they were worthless," he explained. "Young men of the village who spent their time in my employ wishing to be skiing by moonlight, or sharing wine with their sweethearts.

"Do you know, one night, I woke up to find a man in my room? He was a mad Canadian. Fortunately, he did not wish me harm. He wanted me to back him in a chain of escargot shops throughout North America."

Can't get away from the damn things, Ron thought. He'd eaten half so far; he stopped now with the fourth one halfway to his lips. "Don't tell me," he said. "McSnails."

The baron shuddered. "He did not quite go so far as to tell me a name, for which I thank God. In any case, the security guards soon came, but I was nonetheless furious. Suppose it had been someone intent on violence?"

Benedetti smiled. "Like the person we are now attempting to deal with." Ron saw the old man turn his gaze slowly toward Romanescu, who until this moment had been sharing the dinner with what seemed to be a brave show of cordiality. Surreptitiously, the Romanian extended the first and third figures of his right hand. The Professor had taught Ron that this was the *mano cornuta,* used throughout southern and Eastern Europe to ward off the evil eye.

"I don't know if any security system," Romanescu said, "would be enough to ward off 'the one we are now attempting to deal with' as you put it, Professor Benedetti. I only pray I am wrong."

"I will tell you of my current precautions," the baron said. "Perhaps it will ease your mind."

Ron had one more snail to take care of. He closed his eyes and fought it down. Now he only hoped nobody would bring him seconds.

The baron was talking. Bragging, rather.

". . . run on electricity, you see, from outside the normal power grid, and run to the house through shielded, underground wires. After the system is armed by Hilaire and his assistant, no one can touch the fence around the property, the gate, or the outside of any of the doors and windows of the château without receiving an electric shock that will stun him severely, perhaps even render him unconscious, and a loud alarm rouses the whole château.

"In addition, if any of the doors or windows *are* opened, even from the inside, an alarm sounds in the security office, and Hilaire and his man are there with guns drawn in virtual seconds."

"We can vouch for that," Janet said. "All we wanted was a little air."

"Forgive me, madame," the baron said. "There is a small lever behind the curtain to the right side of the window that switches off the alarm and electricity for that window. This allows you to open the window at will. I was remiss not to tell you—I had forgotten the American passion for fresh air."

It was time for the next course. Ron braced himself for squid or something, but it turned out to be veal in some sort of lemon sauce, and it was delicious. He made it through the rest of the meal with delight.

They met after dinner in Benedetti's room. *This* was a place that could stand to have a window open. The old man must have stayed in here all day, and smoked about sixty-seven cigars.

Ron wrinkled his nose, but kept silent. He dared a lot with the Professor, but two things he wasn't about risk doing were to try to get the old man to give up his beloved guinea-stinkers, and to try to stir him to activity when they were on a case. The latter wouldn't have made any sense, anyway. The activity that counted took place in back of that sloping brow. Besides, the old man was perfectly capable of action when he was ready.

He'd certainly made a lot of progress at the easel today, at any rate. The painting of the werewolf carrying off the young girl was done, signed as usual with a stylized "B." The Professor had propped it on a chair in the corner.

Benedetti saw Ron and Janet looking. "I believe it is a decent job for one of my representational efforts. Do you think the baron would care to have it?"

"If he doesn't, *Grave Tales* will buy it for a cover illustration."

"I don't think so," Janet said.

"Sure they would. They love werewolf stuff."

"I mean, I don't think it's wise to offer it to the baron. At least not now. He's tense, he's worn out, and he's hypersensitive about this werewolf idea. I was surprised when he invited Romanescu into the house, since he started the whole thing."

"For some men," Benedetti said, "the obligations of hospitality outweigh any other consideration. Benac has invited, in a sense, the whole world of science to be his guest. It is a heavy burden, and would be even without a murderer running loose."

The old man turned to his easel. A stretched canvas sat waiting for him. *"Va bène,"* he said. "I will keep the werewolf for now." He opened a jar of gesso, and began preparing the canvas. "But what have you accomplished today, my friends?"

Almost simultaneously, Ron and Janet said, "Don't ask."

Benedetti smiled. The broad brush spread the gesso, whitening and smoothing the rough gray canvas. "But I do ask. Have I failed, then, to teach you that one may never dismiss a fact as worthless?"

"One may form a humble opinion, Maestro," Ron said.

Benedetti nodded. He lit a cigar, which in that room was superfluous. Ron could see Janet's eyes getting red.

"Would you like me to open a window, Maestro?" he said. "Now that I know how to do it, I mean."

The Professor consented. Ron went over, threw the switch, and opened the window. It was a beautiful night, and Ron spent a few seconds enjoying it. Then, because he was a detective, and because he'd been trained, he noticed things.

"The moon," he said, "is now in the phase known as waning gibbous. No longer full. If that's any comfort to anybody."

Uncharacteristically, Janet grunted. "It'll help a few of my crowd get to sleep," she said. Her voice was sardonic. That wasn't like her, either.

"I have another humble opinion, Maestro."

The old man spread gesso. "Be sure to keep them humble, *amico*. Humility is the key to discovering the truth. Huxley said, 'Sit down before the fact as a little child.' Of course, one must use one's imagination, but we must never hesitate to change theories when the facts insist we do so."

Ron looked down from the window. "My humble opinion is that the baron's security system is woefully negligent against an inside job. We're about ten, twelve feet from some soft grass below. An army could sneak in here in delivery trucks during the day, disguised as giant escargots, or something—"

"That reminds me, dear," Janet said. "You cleaned your plate. I'm so proud of you."

"Let's not talk about that, okay?"

Benedetti and Janet laughed. Ron went on. "Anyway, they could get smuggled in, then secrete themselves around the grounds until after dark. A guest in one of these rooms turns off the switch, throws one of these fancy sheets out the window, and they all climb in. They overpower the two guards, turn off the alarm, loot the place and drive out through the main gate. Benac would probably sleep through the whole thing."

"Perhaps," Benedetti said. "But we were not brought here to be security consultants. I find it hard to generate much concern over the prospect of an assault in force. Do you think it likely?"

"No, Maestro, it's just that people put in security systems and feel invulnerable. I think they wind up more at risk."

"And the more impregnable one makes a house," Benedetti said, "the more one's life resembles that of a prisoner. Now. Are you, or are you not, going to tell me what you learned today?"

"You go first," Janet said.

Ron pulled a notebook out of his pocket. He sat down. "Dr. Jacques Spaak," Ron said. "I spent some time with him, most of which was taken up by him trying to explain to me what a gluon was supposed to be. He was a lot better at outlining his theory of the crime."

Ron pushed his glasses back up his nose. "You know the background on this guy. Mixed parentage from a society that's polarized—in a mostly nonviolent, but still acrimonious way. He's single, wrapped up in his work, kind of a loner. This 'Task Force' business is the greatest thing that's ever happened to him. A little footnote to this case is that our killer, whoever it turns out to be, has probably done Jacky Spaak more good than a battalion of psychologists—sorry, love—ever could.

"He is also just plain nuts over private eyes. He grinned and wiggled like a puppy when I got out my notebook. And he has a theory."

"He has a theory," the old man echoed.

"He sure does," Ron said. "And the hell of it is, it's not that bad. I don't believe it, but at least it's conceivable that events in the known universe could work out the way he suspects."

"Does this mean," Benedetti said with just the *slightest* trace of asperity, "that I am at last to be allowed to know what he said?"

Ron grinned. "Come on, Maestro, you know you always insist on context. The context in this case is that Spaak, with absolutely no experience in what I would call the real world, has taken Raymond Chandler and Ross Macdonald for gospel."

"Which means?"

"Which means rich people are either teaming up to destroy little people, or they're destroying little people in an effort to get at each other. Spaak likes the latter one, in this case. It's the brainy Belgian's notion that some other super-rich plutocrat—or is that redundant?"

"Moderately," the Professor said. "Go on."

"That somebody in the baron's income bracket is orchestrating these killings, the real target being Benac. The idea is that if he is discredited, his empire will totter, stock will fall, and the rival can swoop up a spare empire."

"At least it sounds *possible,*" Janet said. "I mean, greed is at least a recognizable human emotion. And I read that the baron is famous for the personal control he keeps over his empire. If the public loses faith in him, his empire could still be in trouble. It's happened before."

Ron shook his head. "I just don't buy it. For one thing, they do business differently in Europe."

Janet rolled her eyes. "Darling, don't try to tell me they're above dirty tricks."

Ron grinned at her. "I wouldn't dream of it, dear. I will tell you, though, that one of the dirty tricks they've come up with that's not legal in the States is to have two kinds of common stock—the voting kind, that the family or individual who founded the company hangs onto for dear life, and the profit-participation-only kind, which they sell to the peons. That way, the founder of the company can still run things like a private fiefdom—witness the baron— while still raising money from the public. I doubt there's five shares of voting stock in the baron's domain that he doesn't control personally. I'll get Paul Levesque to tell me for sure tomorrow, but I know how I'm betting."

"Why doesn't Spaak know this?" Janet asked. "He's a European. We're not."

"The man reads literally nothing but scientific reports and American private eye novels. What's he going to learn about business from that? He'll learn that all business deals are fueled by blackmail or violence; all millionaires have beautiful, sad, lonely daughters; and if you go to work for an oil company, you are bound to kill a few people before too long.

"That's the real reason I don't buy his theory, Maestro. Nobody needs to do business like that any more, if they ever did. Even back in the days of the so-called robber barons, they blew up rival oil wells, tore up competitors' railroad tracks. They didn't go around offing innocent civilians in the hopes of driving stock prices down. Today, there are too many legal ways to make money—I'm only talking legal, here, not necessarily savory—to go in for the real nasty stuff."

Benedetti puffed his cigar. "Excellent, *amico*. I tend to agree. Still, I ask: did Dr. Spaak have a candidate for this insatiable businessman?"

"Alexandre Caderousse."

"Interesting. Obvious, but interesting."

"Yeah," Ron said. "He's one of the few up there in the baron's league, and I gather from conversations with Levesque that they've always more or less hated each other."

"Innocent—of murder—as he may be," the Professor said, "I believe a talk with Monsieur Caderousse might prove fruitful."

"You'll have to go to Paris to do it," Ron said.

Benedetti smiled. "One rarely needs an added induce-
ment to go to Paris. We shall see. It won't be tomorrow—
Hans Goetz's widow is coming from Germany tomorrow; I
am to interview her personally. I still feel a lack in my
understanding of the first victim. No one has anything but
praise for the man—it seems almost as if he were a perfect
victim, singled out for sacrifice."

"Well," Janet said. "That's one I didn't hear today."

"Ah, yes, my dear. I am most eager to hear what you
did hear today."

Janet smiled wearily. "I'll summarize, first, Professor.
Then if you want it in more detail, I'll give it to you. I guess
I can stand it if you can."

Janet's notebook was about three times the size of
Ron's. "Before I left the office they let me use, I made a
table of trends of opinion. It broke down remarkably along
geographic lines.

"Southern Europeans—Greeks, Italians, Spaniards—
thought it was the CIA, working out some screwy plan.
Arabs and Chinese liked the CIA, too, but they like the
idea that somehow Goetz and de Blois were in the plot,
whatever it was, and have now been killed to shut them up.
By this theory, Romanescu is still in a lot of danger, and
should be protected."

"Maybe I ought to go tell him not to open his window," Ron said.

Janet made a face. "Maybe you should, at that. Romanescu could be in a lot of danger for reasons other than
having been in a CIA plot."

"How so?"

"He still is the only witness, after all."

Benedetti looked at the blank white canvas, dabbed a

little more gesso in one corner, then screwed the top back on the jar. *"Va bène,"* he said. "I'll begin again in the morning." He turned to Janet. "You may be right, *amica*. If the killer, as I am theorizing, is not insane, he must realize that after all these days Dr. Romanescu will have told all he has to tell and that there would be nothing to be gained by killing him. Still, we must guard against the possibility that Niccolo Benedetti is mistaken."

"No matter how unlikely that is," Ron deadpanned.

The Professor gave no sign of having recognized a joke. "Precisely," he said. "I personally will ring Dr. Romanescu's room as soon as we are done here. Please go on, Janet."

Janet sighed. "Okay, where was I? The Southern Europeans like the CIA. There was a lot of that from the Northern Europeans, too—depending on where in the political spectrum they came from. The Eastern Europeans to a man—I should say to a person—think it's a last-ditch attempt by the KGB to reestablish the Iron Curtain. The Russians asked not to be quoted directly."

She returned to her notes. "Let's see . . . Americans, Canadians, British, and Australians lean toward your common-or-garden variety homicidal maniac, with scattered votes for the CIA from those farthest left.

"Here's the best part. A lot of the Africans, and quite of few of the Pacific Island people, think it might really be a werewolf."

"Janet, come on, these people are *scientists,* no matter where they come from."

"Don't be such a racist, dear."

"Me? You're the one—"

"I'm the one who's not finished talking yet. To me,

these people make the most sense of anything I've heard yet. These people are scientists, yes. They are *not* telling me the murders were carried out by a shape-changing super- natural being that could only be killed with a silver bullet or whatever.

"These are people from societies where the belief in magic still plays a major part of life for large portions of the population. One Zimbabwean was telling me how a tribal medicine man he remembered as a child would work the village up with dancing and chanting (and maybe some drugs, he wasn't sure of that) and become a leopard. Whether he convinced himself, or just playacted, he never broke character, and had to be chained up for three or four days until the Leopard Spirit was satisfied.

"Even in western cultures, lycanthropy is a rare but documented mental condition. I was going to start checking up on it tomorrow."

"Ottima idea," Benedetti said. "Excellent idea. We have been too passive on this case. I have allowed us to be."

"We've only been here a couple of days, Maestro," Ron said.

"It doesn't matter. We are here to fight the evil in this place, not to wait for it to come to us. Let us be vigorous. Let us chase up any path, no matter if it be a blind alley. Let us cause things to happen."

The Professor smoothed his hair. He looked about fifteen years younger than he had at the beginning of the evening. "And now," he said, "let us get a good night's rest, and attack the problem tomorrow."

Ron and Janet allowed as how that sounded good to them. Ron reminded the Professor to caution Dr. Roma- nescu, then he and Janet returned to their room and got ready for bed. Ron turned off the window alarm and let in some cool Alpine night air. Janet joined him. She looked up at the moon for a moment.

"What condition did you say the moon was in?" she asked.

"Waning gibbous," Ron said.

"Looks pretty full to me," she said.

15

The Romanian lay awake on his bed and wondered without really caring what the people of Mont-St.-Denis thought of Ion Romanescu.

Did they think him mad because of his outburst on the mountainside? Let them. If he was mad, he was making the most of it, cosseted in the baron's château, not exposed to the inevitible risk the rest of the community assumed.

Perhaps they thought him a coward.

It was true he had been frightened. The shock of the first attack (he never said it, but "of the Werewolf" lingered in the air every time he spoke the phrase) was something he would remember the rest of his life. The sudden feeling of being doomed, trapped. The panic as he sought a way out. The pain and blood as he felt desperate nails clawing his cheek. The sudden elation when he realized that, against all odds, he was going to survive after all. He had told all this in these very words to Professor Benedetti, earlier in the day, with an unfeigned sincerity and truthfulness that amazed him.

He had told Benedetti that, too.

He had been frightened, then, and he still knew fear. Both the day and night held their terrors for him. Romanescu could only lie low and hope those who might pursue him found other things to occupy themselves.

No. He would do—he was already doing more than hoping. He was, after all, a survivor. He had survived the years of dictatorship in his homeland, and the bloody end of that dictatorship. That hadn't been easy, either. Neither was this, but there were things he could do. He would ask to leave Mont-St.-Denis and OSI, perhaps to stay in England or the United States. Surely they must soon let him go, on grounds of health, if not the putative danger he was in. He would of course promise to be available to return for further questioning, or to testify at a trial, if anybody ever arrested anyone in this case.

He had to make many decisions, some quite soon. What would help him; what would keep him here exposed to danger?

Romanescu made his first decision. He knew Benedetti had advised him otherwise, but the Romanian wanted to show he was not completely intimidated either by the danger or by the Great Man's warnings. He switched off the alarm and opened the window, then went back to his bed.

He never even bothered to look at the moon. His astronomical contributions to this gathering, never destined for greatness in any event, were now over.

Jacky Spaak could barely contain his excitement. This was too good. He was on an adventure worthy of Sam Spade, a middle-of-the-night meeting with a key informant, with secrecy the key word.

Of course, Jacky had to concede to himself that the adventure did lack one element—danger. He knew well the voice that had spoken to him over the phone (indeed, with television and radio news, it was unlikely anyone in town could fail to recognize it), and he knew that this was one person—perhaps *the* one person on the whole mountain —with whom he might feel completely safe.

The meeting place, too, had been selected with care. In the unlikely (or more realistically, impossible) event that his informant wished to do him harm, he still wouldn't be able to reach Jacky to do it. Furthermore, help was no more than an arm's reach away.

Jacky turned off the alarm clock in his room at a quarter to three, five minutes before it had been due to go off. He had been too excited to sleep, anyway. He dressed in a soft black suit, with crepe-soled black brushed leather shoes. He knotted his black knit tie, then lit a cigarette and looked at himself in the mirror.

Not bad, he thought, suppressing the urge to giggle. Still, he thought, he might as well indulge himself. This was the one night when he could put aside the pencil-pushing reality of his life and act like, seem like, *be* a private eye. He might as well enjoy it to the full, and dress the part.

He regretted that the night was too warm for a trench coat. He regretted that he did not in fact *own* a trench coat. That was something he would have to rectify at his earliest convenience.

He walked quietly down the back stairs on his crepe soles. The word "gumshoe" resounded happily in his heart. Outside the hotel, he made his way to his old German Opel, climbed in, and started the motor. The muffler was bad, and the popping noises echoed strangely in the quiet streets.

As he drove by the Prefecture of Police, his conscience gave a twinge. He was not, as much as he enjoyed imagining it, a Private Eye, and this could be vital information he was about to pick up. The police should be told—

No! They should not be told. The very importance of the information made that imperative. Jacky's informant had said that if anyone learned of their meeting, the informant would deny the phone call had ever taken place, and would maintain silence forever. There was information to impart, and it would be imparted to Dr. Jacky Spaak and no other, to do with as he judged right. The informant *trusted* Jacky, it was that simple.

Jacky parked his car a few hundred yards away from his objective. The way the road curved, he could just see the topmost spires of Château Benac. He began walking toward it. He did not however, approach the main gate, but veered off to the right, toward the east wing of the building. He began counting the stone pillars of the fence, as he had been instructed.

It was a longer walk than he had expected; the château and grounds were huge, considering it was perched on the side of a mountain. ". . . Thirteen." Jacky walked on. "Fourteen." He was beginning to get breathless. "Seventeen . . . eighteen."

It should be right about here. . . .

"Spaak!" hissed a voice from the darkness. It was a good name for hissing.

"Ah!" Jacky said aloud.

"Quiet!" the voice cautioned him.

"Sorry," Jacky whispered. He was glad he remembered to speak English. That had been another one of the conditions. "I'm happy you're here. I was beginning to get nervous."

"This will be easier if you come closer," the voice said.

Jacky laughed self-consciously and stepped forward. A claw lashed out of the darkness and caught him under the chin. He tried to grab for it, but the claw was in deep, in the softness of his throat, lifting him, pulling him.

It was over in seconds. Jacky Spaak fell to the ground outside the fence, eyes open, facing the guest wing of the baron's château. The claws were disengaged from his throat. Retreating footsteps made no sound on the soft grass.

Despite the fact that he was descended from bakers as far back as the records in the church could show, Antoine Martin, the latest *fils* in the very excellent firm of Martin et Fils Pâtisserie, could never quite reconcile himself to rising so early in the morning.

He would much rather remain awake through the night, mixing, kneading, baking, but his father, also Antoine, would have none of it. Once—*once*—when he was fourteen, the younger Antoine had allowed the brioches to burn. The son's penance was now in its seventh year, and showed no sign of abating.

"As a baker," father repeatedly said, "you are a good truck driver!"

So the son rose in the darkness, loaded up the truck, and made delivery to the hotels in town, to the châteaus of the rich. It was the honor of Martin et Fils to be supplier of bread and pastries to Monsieur le Baron himself. It was a matter of young Antoine's personal honor that he had never been late with a delivery, through snow or rain or anything nature might send.

Then he scrupulously returned to town, and opened the shop, which he manned until the afternoon. He had earned no praise from his father for this, but no blame either. Young Antoine knew it was a matter of time before his exile would be over. If Martin et Fils were to continue, the *fils* must know how to bake!

As he drove along the roadway that led to the trades-man's entrance at the rear of the château, Antoine noticed a splash of red across the road. It did not occur to him that the puddle might really be *blood* until he had nearly driven in it.

He pulled the truck over to the roadside. He opened the glove compartment and removed a large knife. He left the truck with a mixture of French compassion—some poor creature has been struck by a car, perhaps it will be necessary to put it out of its misery—and French practical-ity—that much blood must mean a deer at least; if it is not too badly mangled, there will be fresh venison for the Mar-tin family.

He followed the blood across the road toward the châ-teau fence. He saw nothing there but what looked like a bundle of rags. He was astonished that the baron's staff would allow such a thing so near the baron's property. Young Antoine would tell them of this when he completed the delivery.

Yet where had the blood come from? Antoine walked closer. He now saw that the bundle of rags was a man, a man who had fallen at an angle, his face toward the fence, his head and neck twisted sideways.

Antoine saw what had happened to that neck. His legs turned to water. He staggered backward until he hit the fence. His body jolted forward with an electric shock.

He fought off the disorientation; he was a strong young man. *"Loup-garou,"* he breathed. "Werewolf."

He crossed himself three times, once each for the Father, Son, and Holy Spirit. Added an extra for St. Denis, patron of France.

If he'd been listening closely, he might have heard bells and sirens from the château, but he could take neither his eyes nor his stunned mind from the sight before him.

16

Though the window alarms at Château Benac sounded only in the guard's office, the alarms from the fence seemed designed to shake the very mountain on which the château sat.

The noise jolted Janet out of a sound sleep. She nudged her husband. "Ron, for God's sake, wake up! Don't you hear that?"

"Hear what?"

"Bells and sirens."

"You always make me hear bells and sirens, baby," he said, and she hit him.

"Someone's set off the alarm," she said. "Wake up."

Ron willed one eyelid up. The other shot open when a man's voice began screaming in terror.

"What's he saying?" Janet demanded.

"Got me," Ron told her. "French stuff. I'm going to see what's going on. You get decent, then stay with the Professor. I'll be back as soon as I can."

Ron had stepped into pants and shoes as he spoke. He grabbed his glasses and pulled on a shirt on the way to the door. "Oh, yeah," he said. "Close the window and turn the alarm back on."

"I will. Be careful."

"Don't worry," Ron said sincerely, and he was gone.

As he sped down the hallway, Ron stopped outside Professor Benedetti's door just as the old man poked his head outside.

"What is this commotion, Ronald? Not your window again, I trust."

"No, Maestro. This is from outside. And there's a man outside screaming. I'm going to investigate."

"Go. I will join you as soon as I am dressed."

"Right," Ron said. He started off.

"Wait!" the old man said.

Ron turned around. "Yes?"

"Check on Dr. Romanescu. Make sure he is all right."

"Right," Ron said again. More proof that the old boy is a genius. They'd been nervous about Romanescu's safety all along; then when a disturbance comes, the guards rush to the site of the alarm (they certainly hadn't shown up here), Ron himself plans to fly to the site of the alarm, and only Benedetti remembers about the most likely target.

Dumb, Gentry, he told himself. Real dumb. The fact that you were sound asleep basking in the afterglow of having made love to your wife was no excuse.

Says you, Ron thought.

He had to wipe the grin off his face as he knocked on Romanescu's doors.

"Dr. Romanescu?"

No answer. He knocked harder and called the name again.

Still no answer. This time he pounded on the door and shouted the Romanian's name.

He tried again, but he was already sizing up the door. Solid oak, hard as iron. Heavy hinges, massive lock. They knew how to build châteaux in those days. This was going to be more than a little difficult to kick in. He'd need a good push off the opposite wall, and the perfect leg piston-action even to have a chance. Probably break his foot in the process.

Probably walk into a room full of trouble, too. Why didn't he answer?

He'd take one last shot at pounding and shouting. He did, sighed, and began backing against the other wall when a voice came from inside the room.

"Yes? Yes? Why are you pounding? What do you want?" The voice was strained, querulous, and breathless at the same time.

"It's Ron Gentry, Doctor. There's been some kind of incident, and I wanted to make sure you're all right."

Ron could hear locks clicking and bolts sliding back. Finally the door opened a little, and one gray eye peeped out.

"An incident? What kind of incident?"

"I'm on my way to find out," Ron told him. "But we thought it would be a good idea to make sure you're okay, first."

"I'm fine. I give you my word. Go away."

"I'd like to see you, sir."

"I am not a vision of loveliness at this hour of the morning, young man."

"Oh," Ron said. Then he dropped his voice to a whisper. "Is there someone in there?" Ron had visions of some maniac, desperado, or terrorist in the room with the old man, holding a gun on him, telling him to make the nosy intruder go away.

"Is there what?" Romanescu demanded. "Someone in here with me?" Amazingly, the old man began to laugh. "No," he said. "There is not. Unfortunately, those days are long past. All right. Come in. If you must."

The door opened wide and Ron stepped in. The commotion could be heard plainly through Romanescu's open window, fluttering a little as the breeze blew the curtain back and forth. The screaming voice had been joined by two stern, angry voices, undoubtedly the baron's guards.

"Forgive me if I seem rude," Romanescu said. He still seemed to be out of breath. "I was sleeping, then suddenly the screaming, the shouting, the bells and sirens—it was like Romania in the bad days. Then when you came pounding on the door and calling my name, I had visions of the secret police!"

Ron felt like a louse. He, who had grown up secure in a free country, had never considered the effect a knock in the night could have on a man who'd spent his adulthood under one of the most repressive regimes in human history.

"You nearly gave me a heart attack," Romanescu went on.

"Look," Ron said, "I'm really sorry, but when Professor Benedetti knew something was up, he told me—"

"It's all right. It is I who should be sorry. When I found out it was only you come for me, and not the secret police, I was so relieved I became—what is the word—surly? Can you understand how that might be?"

"Sure," Ron told him. "It happens all the time."

Ron listened. The shouting and screaming were still going on. "They should have calmed down a little by now," he said. "May I look out your window?"

It was Ron's turn to be rude. He didn't wait for permission. He went to the window and swept the curtain aside with one arm.

"Uh-oh," he said.

It so happened that Romanescu's window was the one closest to the part of the fence that had been tampered with.

Ron could see now, under the perimeter lamp, the baron's two guards being held at bay by a wild-looking young man with a knife. And all this was being played out on the shores of a veritible ocean of red liquid. Ron had the nauseous suspicion that it was blood.

He turned to Romanescu. "He might not be alone," he said.

"Who might not be alone?"

"It doesn't matter. Just lock the window after I'm gone. Find somebody to stay with—the baron, Levesque, a servant, it doesn't matter. We'll keep you safe, okay?"

"Yes. I'm in full agreement with that. But what—?"

Ron was up on the windowsill. He turned, and grabbed the inside of the sill with both hands. "Quickest way," he said. The he slipped off.

Ron dangled by his fingertips for a few seconds, then let go. He reminded himself before he did to bend his knees on landing, and was glad a split second later that he had taken his own advice, because there was decorative gravel against the building under the window, and while that stuff would give a little with impact, it wouldn't give much.

Ron tested his ankles, found he hadn't done either of them any damage, then took off across the yard.

The place was full of hazards. There was a wet spot by a garden hose outlet in the middle of the grounds. Just past that, Ron tripped and went down when he stepped on something hard. He cursed, reached around for what he'd tripped on, and found it. A three-pronged garden cultivator. Ron supposed he should have been glad he'd stepped on the handle—those nasty, curved prongs would have gone right through his shoe and foot at the speed he'd been traveling—but he didn't feel especially grateful, just frustrated. He flung the cultivator back in the direction of the gardener's toolshed, where it undoubtedly belonged, then continued. He was more cautious, this time.

By the time Ron got to within sixty or seventy feet of the fence, he decided he was grateful for having tripped, after all. Slowing down had given him time to think, and thinking had shown him the folly of charging up like the U.S. cavalry when all the action was on the other side of the fence. He stuck to the shadows, watched and listened. He was able to get right up to the fence about twenty feet from the scene of the action without anyone there noticing him. They were, after all, preoccupied.

One of the men was a baker. At least, he was dressed in white like a baker, and he was standing in front of a bakery truck, and that was a bread knife he had at the throat of one of the Baron's Finest. The other of the baron's guards was pointing a gun at the two of them.

The fourth man present was the source of the redness. The shadows were such that Ron couldn't make out many details, but the man was obviously messily dead just inches from the baron's fence.

Ron didn't speak French, but he knew enough of tones and faces and body language to figure out what was going on.

The baker was the screamer. His position was that if the other guy didn't drop the gun *this second,* his partner would be sliced up better than a fresh, Sunday morning *pain.*

The guy with the gun was the shouter. He was the baron's guard, goddammit, and nobody would get away from him, and if he didn't release his hostage *this second,* he would fill the air with bullets, and to hell with the consequences.

It hadn't been audible at the house, but the guy with

the knife on his neck was contributing to the colloquy, as well. He was a moaner, and his position was, Jesus, please, get me the hell out of this.

Ron knew that if he (or somebody else sane, a kind of person of which there seemed to be a short supply at the moment) didn't do something soon, there was going to be a bloodbath here. This would be unfortunate on its own, of course, but also, Ron knew, because it would screw up the investigation of the murder that had already been committed. Ron hadn't had a close look at anything yet, but he felt in his bones that that one had all the earmarks of the work of the boy they'd been looking for.

Ron decided to scale the fence. It wouldn't be too bad, except for the spikes on the top. He didn't have to worry about the alarm, because that was still clanging and shrieking away, back at the house. And the shock mechanism had to be turned off, or the guards couldn't have gotten out. There was a slight risk of the guard with the gun spotting him and letting him have it, but Ron didn't think it was likely that man's eyes would waver from the bread knife even for a split second.

Speaking of splits, Ron split his pants going over the fence, but he made it. He sprinted silently across the road, and dove into a ditch that lined the other side. Then he made his way along the ditch until he was behind the bread truck.

He climbed to road level, then half ran, half crawled up to the truck, and slid underneath it.

Something hot dripped on Ron's face. He'd have to tell the baker he had a leaky crankcase. Ron was glad he hadn't grabbed a good shirt as he inched forward toward the street-side edge of the truck, and the oil drew a black stripe down his back.

When he got to the point where one more shove
would push his head out from under the truck, he stopped
and looked at feet. He wouldn't have much leverage in this
position—if he guessed wrong, that guard was going to
wind up with the knife in his throat.

Ron had to picture the scene in his mind, and reverse
it. Okay. The baker had the knife in his right hand, so . . .

Ron reached out with both hands, grabbed the
rightmost of the pair of legs clad in white (the gray legs
were the guard's), and yanked hard, as though trying to
pull the man clear under the truck.

The screaming abruptly switched to a cry of shock,
and the hand with the knife in it came down to the ground
as the baker tried to keep his balance. Ron let go of the leg
with one hand, and reached for the knife hand.

Then he remembered one thing he hadn't thought of
—the other guard had been dying to shoot this guy for at
least five minutes. Now that he was down and the hostage
was released, would he cut loose?

Ron wished he knew the French for "Don't shoot!"
"Défense de Fumer," meant no smoking, which was close,
but probably wouldn't get the message across. So Ron stuck
to English, and hoped that the guy with the gun had seen
enough American movies. *Everybody* in France had seen
dozens of American movies.

All the while, of course, he kept pulling on the baker's
right hand and leg, to keep the guy off balance.

Finally, Ron heard a crunch, and the baker fell into
Ron's visible universe—a two-foot-high slot between the
truck and the pavement. He fell facing Ron, and the American could see that the young man was glassy-eyed, but
breathing.

Ron scrambled back out from under the truck, and walked around to join Benac's warriors.

The guy who'd been held at knifepoint greeted him like a small-scale recreation of Normandy greeting the American troops, falling on his neck, kissing him, blessing him between sobs, burying him in thank-yous. He did everything but ask for cigarettes and nylon stockings.

The shorter guy, the one with the gun, was slightly less effusive, but he did grin wide and pump Ron's hand a few times.

"Great," Ron said, trying to disengage his arm. "It's all right. I was glad to do it. I regret that I had but one shirt to give to a gallant ally. Now will you please let go, and let me see if this guy's all right?"

They shook their heads sadly, and pointed to the figure by the fence. The one with the gun (the gun still had a little wad of the baker's hair sticking to it) drew a finger across his throat. The other guy shuddered.

"Not him," Ron said. "I know he's—"

Ron had walked closer to get a better look at the body. When he got a good look at the face, he said, "Holy Jesus." He looked again. It was Spaak, all right—"coordinator" of the OSI participants' investigation. He wanted to be a private eye, Ron thought. The poor bastard fell on his first case. He coordinated everybody into an incredible mess. The more Ron thought about it, the worse it got. This doesn't make any goddamn sense at all.

Where the hell are you, Professor? Ron thought.

With an almost physical effort, Ron pulled his eyes away from the dead Belgian, and walked over to the baker, whose name was possibly Martin, judging from the writing on the truck, and looked at him.

He was out, and from the look of him, would be out for hours. Blood was still oozing from his scalp, so at least he wasn't dead.

"Nice job," Ron said.

The guy with the gun agreed. "Nighzh zhob," he said, nodding. *"Très bien."*

"He might be able to tell us something."

"Très bien," the guard said, still smiling and nodding. Ron resolved at that moment never to set foot in a non-English-speaking country again.

"If you haven't left him brain-damaged."

More smiles and nods. *"Très bien."*

That was when Ron decided none of his descendants would ever set foot in a non-English-speaking country, either. "Did it occur to one of you mental giants," he asked, "to phone the police?"

Ron held an invisible receiver to his ear. "Telephone," he said. "The police."

Faces lit up. "Ahh," the guards breathed. *"Téléphone la police!"*

"Oui!" Terrific, Ron thought. I'm learning French. "Did you?"

Faces fell. *"Non."* There were sad shrugs.

"Where the hell are you, Professor?"

This time, he said it aloud.

17

"Here I am, *amico,*" the familiar voice said.

Ron looked up. He was about to ask what took the old man so long, but one look at him answered that question. The Professor had shaved, dressed himself in a suit and an immaculate white shirt, and taken the time to tie his bow tie just right.

Ron should have known. The old man would never be content just to be a guy who'd had a body dumped on his host's doorstep in the middle of the night. He had to be *Niccolo Benedetti* under all conceivable circumstances.

"Have *you* called the police?" Ron asked.

"Indeed I have," the Professor said. "And seen Romanescu and Mrs. Gentry safe within the baron's private apartment—where the security is considerably better."

"You mean he has three stooges there, instead of two?"

"You do the men wrong, Ronald. There has been no breach of the baron's security."

"But—" Ron began. Then he thought about it and saw that the old man was right. All the nastiness had taken place outside the fence. The baron and his guests may have had their sleep disturbed, but anything else Ron had found to peeve him about this little episode he had walked into voluntarily.

"You're right, Maestro," he conceded.

Benedetti smiled. "The day I make a habit of being wrong, I shall cease to be the Maestro."

"Have you seen who the dead man is?"

"I have."

"You're taking it calmly."

"One should train one's emotions not to fill the gap when the mind is a blank, my friend."

"In other words, you don't know what the hell is going on here either."

"In a word, no."

"Well, let me see if this guy is ever going to be in a position to tell us anything. Ask one of the stalwarts there if I can borrow his flashlight."

The Professor spoke softly in French, and the guard Ron had rescued ran to him and pressed his flashlight into his hand like one of the faithful trying to get the pope to touch his rosary. Ron took it from him with a smiled thanks, but he was beginning to get uneasy. As he saw to the baker, he could hear Benedetti questioning the guards.

When he was done, he stood and turned to Benedetti, who turned from his interrogations to ask, "Well?"

"His pupils are equal and reactive. That's a good sign, but I'm no doctor, and he needs one. Want to go back to the house and phone for one? Or should I send Mr. Gratitude, here?"

"It won't be necessary," the Professor said. Ron could hear new sirens through the din still coming from the château. "The police can call for one much quicker on their radios."

Two cars pulled up, about two minutes apart. The first contained two uniformed local constables, who very efficiently put up tape around the scene of the crime, took everyone's name, and began to get stories.

The second contained a driver, Prefect of Police Diderot, and Captain Marx of the Sûreté.

Etienne Diderot looked in alarm at Captain Samuel Marx. The Alsatian always gave the impression of suppressed anger; now the anger was at the surface. Marx was so mad that smoke seemed to be coming from him.

A second look showed Diderot that smoke *was* coming from him. Or rather from the cigarette that dangled from his mouth.

Diderot, who was beginning to feel some pique at the arrogant man Paris had sent him to replace the charming de Blois, spoke roughly to his colleague.

"Captain," he said brusquely. "The cigarette. Not here."

Marx must have been very angry indeed to have forgotten a rule so basic in criminal investigation—No Smoking at The Crime Scene.

Marx took the cigarette out of his mouth, glared at it as if he'd caught it trespassing, threw it to the road, and stomped on.

Diderot watched him stomp on. The prefect was about to say something, but thought better of it. He shrugged, picked up Marx's cigarette, crushed it out, and brought it back to the car. He wondered what could be the matter with the Sûreté man. Smoking wasn't forbidden at a crime scene for health reasons—it was because cigarettes and matches themselves often proved to be such excellent clues, providing everything from a suspect's blood type to his

manual preference. It was only wise not to go burying possibly valuable evidence with worthless confusion of your
own manufacture.

One of Diderot's men passed by, saluted, then used his
car radio to call for an ambulance. When he'd done with
that, the prefect got a brief report of what was going on
here.

Madness. Simply madness. He didn't care what the
vaunted Professor Benedetti said, there was a madman at
work here, and it was going to be hell to catch him.

When he ducked under the barricade, the prefect
could hear Marx talking to Gentry. Perhaps berating him
was a better word.

"I know Americans like to meddle," Marx was saying.
"But this is too much. Physically assaulting suspects! Questioning witnesses before the police get here! Tampering
with evidence! There are strict laws in the Republic of
France about those things, Monsieur Gentry."

Diderot could see the young American was controlling
himself only with great effort.

"Yeah. Americans love to meddle. I meddled here the
way we meddled in World War Two. That is, I bailed your
ass out of a desperate situation. Ask the guard. If I hadn't
done what I did, the Republic of France would have had its
population decreased by at least one more, possibly two. As
for assault, I'm not the one who clobbered him. As for
tampering with evidence, you're out of your mind. As for
anything else, take it up with the Professor. He's standing
right over there."

"You will answer my questions," Marx snarled. "You
do not amuse me."

"Shame," Gentry said. "I think you're funny as hell.
Furthermore, you haven't asked me a single question. And

even furthermore, I was awakened out of a sound sleep, and risked my life to keep this situation from becoming any worse than it already is. Okay, I took a job and I'm doing it; we can skip the parade under the Arc de Triomphe. But I'll be damned if I'll take any abuse about it."

Marx opened his mouth, but Gentry cut him off.

"As of now," he said, "as far as you are concerned, I have amnesia and a severe case of laryngitis. Send me Diderot, or someone else who can ask a civil question, and we'll see. In the meantime, take it up with the Professor."

"I think not—" Marx began, but Gentry had turned away from him. Marx lifted his arm, as though to clap the young man on the shoulder and turn him around.

Diderot saw the tension, the tautness in Gentry's muscles, and was almost hoping the Sûreté man would do it, for he would surely be rewarded with a punch in the mouth.

Diderot knew that, considering his own frustration with the Mysterious Professor Benedetti and his assistants, this desire was somewhat illogical, but he spent more time in the company of Marx, and therefore was even more annoyed with him. For the love of God, the man didn't even know how to behave at a crime scene!

Unfortunately, Captain Marx must have seen the same tension in Gentry's manner, because Diderot saw him lower his arm again, and, following the young American's advice, turn to Professor Benedetti, who was standing near the fence, grinning.

"So, Professor," Marx said. His voice was oily. Diderot was learning to hate an Alsatian accent, even when it spoke English. "It seems I am to take it up with you."

"Take what up?" Benedetti asked.

"The matter of your assistant's misconduct."

"I think my assistant answered the charges master-

fully, though I do agree with you that Americans tend to
meddle. But he has committed no misconduct. If you had
bothered to investigate before arriving and throwing
around accusations backed by nothing but insecurity and
chauvinism, you would have discovered that for yourself."

"His manner and language were disrespectful."

"Ahh," Benedetti said, and spread his hands. "On that
count, I must apologize on my young friend's behalf."

"I should hope—" Marx began.

"He has," Benedetti went on, "never learned the art of
feigning respect for officious fools."

Marx narrowed his eyes. "Are you suggesting I am
acting like a fool?"

"Not at all," Benedetti said good-naturedly. "A suggestion is a statement that lacks conclusive evidence."

Diderot began to laugh. He corked it with a fist, but it
wanted to bubble loose, like agitated champagne. He did
his best to turn it into a cough instead, none too success-
fully. Diderot suspected he'd be added to the list of Captain
Marx's enemies, but he suspected this was worth it.

"I am a fool, then," Marx said. "What have *you* done
since you have come here, except interfere with my investigation?"

"*Your* investigation? Has M. Diderot retired?"

"Not yet, Professor," Diderot said.

Marx was concentrating on the Professor.

"Do you honestly believe," he said, "that Dr. Spaak
would be dead right now if you and your Americans hadn't
encouraged him in his insane scheme to investigate these
crimes?"

"Since I have no idea why Dr. Spaak was killed, I
simply cannot answer your question."

"But we see *how* he was killed, don't we? With his throat torn out. And this time, on your very doorstep."

"Even allowing for hyperbole," Benedetti said, "this is the doorstep of Monsieur le Baron, not mine."

Benedetti's grin became more catlike than ever. "Is it my understanding, Captain Marx, that you wish me to withdraw from this investigation?"

"To put it mildly, yes."

Benedetti gave him a little bow. "Then you must persuade the baron to dismiss me. Now, if you'll excuse me, I'll await further—and I hope competent—questioning at the château."

"You can't leave."

"I must. This is a crime scene, after all, and I feel the need of a cigar."

18

Next morning, Paul Levesque volunteered to drive Benedetti and Mr. and Mrs. Gentry to the Hotel Racine for their
appointment with Mme. Goetz, thereby becoming the high-
est-paid chauffeur in France.

He did so for two reasons. First of all, when the police
had awakened him at the crack of dawn to question him
about the events of the night, Levesque had been completely at a loss. This was not supposed to happen. He was
supposed to know everything that concerned the baron, *and*
have at least one idea to offer on what to do about it.

It was not, of course, his fault, nor was it the fault of
the baron himself, who was similarly in the dark. The men
slept in another part of the château; their quarters were
soundproofed; and neither one of them had the Anglo-
Saxon passion for fresh air at night, the very thought of
which made Levesque want to shudder.

By taking the baron's big Jaguar and driving the investigators to town, Levesque hoped to learn something
that could be of use in seeing to the well-being of the
baron's affairs.

The other reason, frankly, was to get away from the
office. Because, Levesque knew, with this latest atrocity,
wolves would infest Mont-St.-Denis in force—wolves of the
press, because this was a story too good to pass up; and

wolves of the world of finance, because the smell of the baron's economic blood was too much to resist.

Both of these hordes of carnivores would descend on Paul Levesque before they did anything else, and if Levesque were unavailable, he might delay their onslaught for a few hours. He could also use the time to gather his own dwindling resources.

There was yet another reason Levesque wanted to be away from the château. He simply could not bear to look the baron in the face. The Olympique Scientifique Internationale was dead, its last signs of life extinguished during the night with the unfortunate Belgian physicist. Even if the scientists could be persuaded to stay, or even *compelled* to stay past the reasonable time the police could keep them for the investigation into this latest death, they would do no work. Levesque was sure it was as true in science as it was in any business. Fearful people do no useful work. Resentful people do their best to sabotage whatever you are managing to accomplish. Levesque had taken no survey, but he was certain that the two most prevalent emotions in Mont-St.-Denis this morning were fear and resentment.

For the first third of the trip, Levesque's passengers provided nothing but yawns. Apparently they had gotten no sleep at all last night.

Finally, Gentry asked a question. He had to speak right through a yawn to get it out. "How long will we have your services, Paul?"

"Oh," Levesque said, "I suppose until fourteen hours. I'm sorry, two o'clock."

"Good. After we're done with Mrs. Goetz, I want to go by police headquarters and pick up the police reports. At least Diderot is still speaking to us."

His wife said, "He seemed to be going out of his way

to be nice, last night. This morning. You know what I mean."

"Diderot is a man of honor," Benedetti said. "And he promised full cooperation. I don't think he is especially pleased with my performance thus far."

"Have you gotten anywhere, Professor?" Levesque asked.

Benedetti's grin was sardonic. "I have completed one painting. And I have begun another."

"I just hope," Gentry began, then had to pause for a yawn. "I just hope that son of a bitch Marx is there when I pick up the reports. I hope he makes a remark. I'll stuff an oily shirt down his throat."

"I don't know what his problem is," Janet said. "Even professional jealousy shouldn't make him *this* hostile."

"Maybe he hates Italians," her husband suggested. "And their friends."

In the rear view mirror, Levesque could see Benedetti scratch his chin. "There were many interesting things about the captain's behavior last night," he said.

"Not just last night," Levesque said, before he could stop himself.

"What do you mean?"

"He has been paying attention to one of your witnesses. Personal attention. He has been—how do you put it —putting a rush on Karin Tebner."

"That's interesting," Ron Gentry said. "I knew he'd had a drink with her, but putting on a rush, how, exactly?"

"The usual way," Levesque told him. "Flowers, dinner, who knows what else." *Ferme la bouche,* Paul, Levesque told himself. This way lay nothing but embarrassment.

"That is interesting," Gentry said. "I expect it will

slow down now that the moon is waning, and the star gazers will be getting back to work, but it's still interesting."

Levesque simply grunted.

Gentry wouldn't let the subject go, however.

"How do you happen to know this?" he asked.

"It is my business to know what's going on. In the baron's interest, you know."

"I didn't ask *why* you know," Gentry said. "I asked *how*."

"There are people in town who keep the baron informed of such things. Hotel clerks and the like."

"I see," Gentry said.

"In fact," Levesque said, relaxing, "Marx was with Dr. Tebner at a local bistro again last night."

"Gee," Gentry said. "That's wonderful. We should sign you up."

"Sign me up?"

"As an operative. A network of informants like yours can be incredibly valuable. And you keep track of these things?"

"For the baron, I do."

"What was Peabody up to last night?"

"Who?"

"Launcelot Peabody. The Brit who worked next to Spaak, discussed theories of the murders with him. He's a witness, now. Maybe a suspect. What do your sources tell you about him?"

"I—ahhh, Monsieur Gentry—well."

"Never mind," Gentry said pleasantly. "I already know what he was doing. He was having what the English call a 'piss-up' for a few friends in his room. They were asked to tone down the drunken noise, several times through the night, so he's got a solid alibi, you see. I have a few sources of my own—I've been spreading the baron's francs around town."

"But if—"

"Okay, *now* I ask why."

Levesque was by now thoroughly confused. "Why what?"

"Why are you so handy with the details of Karin Tebner's life?"

"I don't have to answer that," Levesque said. He sounded petulant, even to himself. "I mean, can that really be important?"

Gentry grinned. "The Professor has an entire little speech covering that point." He turned to the old man. "You want to give it to him, Professor, or should I?"

Benedetti said, "You do it; I shall see how well you have listened."

" 'In the humility which is the only proper attitude for an investigator,' " Gentry quoted, " 'we must never judge the importance of isolated facts. We must let logic and events determine that, and accept their dictates meekly.' How was that?"

"I believe I usually say, 'meekly accept their dictates,' " the old man said. "Seriously, Monsieur Levesque, we—all of us—are in a dire situation here. I have faith that the answer exists, but I cannot say from where the true indication of the way to it may come. The fact you wish to hold back may be of vital importance."

"It's not what you think," Levesque said. How could he have put himself in this situation?

"I think nothing," Benedetti said. "I only ask."

Levesque knew he had no one to blame but himself. He had rendered the situation hopeless by now, in any case.

He decided to accept the thing with a humorous fatalism. That was what was expected of a Frenchman, after all. "Very well. It is a matter perhaps too simple to be deduced. I have been interested in Mademoiselle Tebner because I have been *interested* in Mademoiselle Tebner."

"Interested?" Gentry asked.

"Interested," Levesque said. "Attracted. Drawn to. Curious about. My English fails me for further synonyms. It is too soon to say 'enamored'; I hardly know the woman. 'Obsessed' is much, much too strong."

Gentry was nodding. " 'Interested' sounds like the right word. Of course."

"I first met her during the selection process, you see," Levesque went on. He told them how he had found her so refreshing. The way she didn't pretend to be anyone but herself. Her unadorned delight with being considered for OSI. The way she seemed completely unaware of her attractiveness. All of it added up to a kind of honesty and openness he had never seen in a European woman.

"I made a mental note to get better acquainted with her at the first possible opportunity," Levesque said. "It will give you some indication of what a failure I am as a stereotypical Frenchman that in the almost four months since OSI began, that opportunity has not presented itself. First there was the organization of the event, then the first days of special problems and chaos, then, just when things were going smoothly, this cursed Werewolf or whatever he is has come along to fill my days. And nights. To say nothing of my regular work.

"Still, I have found, and still do frequently find myself thinking of the woman, and feeling a little better about the world in general. When the murders started, and she was the one who discovered the first body, I made it a point to use my local network to keep myself informed of her activities."

"There," Gentry said. "That wasn't so bad, was it?"

"I feared you wouldn't understand."

"I understand better than you know."

Benedetti interrupted. "You say she spent last evening with Captain Marx?"

"Till about midnight, yes. Then she took the funicular and went to work, believe it or not. She must be one of the few scientists who are still bothering to do that."

"Spaak was killed long after midnight. I heard the medical examiner telling Diderot."

Levesque heard Benedetti lean back against the leather seat. "But you see, Monsieur Levesque," the old man said, "Your interest in the young lady has had a very positive result. She should be grateful to you."

"She doesn't know. What do you mean, she should be grateful to me?"

"Well, pending confirmation, of course, from the police reports and from your informants, you have provided the young lady with an alibi, something she lacked for the first two murders."

"You don't suspect—"

"Let me simply say that it is a pleasure in a case of this kind to be able to declare even one person absolutely innocent. In this instance our joy is doubled—we have taken the first step toward establishing the alibi of Captain Marx as well."

"He wasn't even *in* Mont-St.-Denis when the first attack took place!" Levesque protested.

"So far as anyone now knows," the Professor conceded. "Still, it is nice to make extra sure. And it is gallant of you to spring so rapidly to the defense of your rival."

Levesque was about to reply to that when he saw they had reached the hotel. He stifled his comment—it would have been something foolishly angry in any case—and pulled up to the curb. As he let his passengers out, he realized that leaving the office to avoid his troubles had been a failure.

19

It occurred to Ron that while he had heard countless ecomiums to the late Herr Professor Doctor Hans Goetz's warmth and wonderfulness, he had heard nothing about his wife past the bare fact of her existence.

Now, as he sat in the parlor of the suite Levesque or a member of his staff had managed to clear for her, watching her talk to Niccolo Benedetti, he was learning about her firsthand.

Gisele Goetz was a lovely woman. Medium height and thin, she had straight blond hair, ice blue eyes, and the bone structure of a fashion model. She wore a severe gray suit over a white blouse, and she had her still-trim legs directly in front of her, tight together, feet planted firmly on the floor. There were wrinkles at the corners of her eyes and mouth, and cords visible in her neck and hands, but she didn't give a damn, and in reality, it wouldn't make much difference. She might have been anything from fifty-five to seventy-five, and she looked great.

Janet, he thought, would be this kind of old lady—not fighting the years, not even giving the years the satisfaction of conceding there was anything to fight about. She'd just go on being herself. It would be a pleasure to grow old with her.

That is, it would be if Janet kept her current attitude. Frau Goetz had the right approach to her appearance, but her demeanor was another matter.

This was a woman on the verge of . . . Ron couldn't say. Breakdown? Hysteria? Violence?

She was perched on the edge of her chair, poised as if to jump up and run away. She was holding her body so tight, her shoulders quivered with the effort. Her voice, which spoke precise, nearly unaccented English, seemed to be coming from outside her, like a spirit voice at a séance.

Benedetti had been introduced by Levesque, who retired from the scene and went to put the car somewhere. The Professor in turn introduced Ron and Janet, but the woman was interested only in the Professor.

Benedetti had his own rules of etiquette. Or rather, he had the usual ones, but he had his own set of rules about when and to whom they *applied*. He could be so brutal to the feelings of a witness as to make Ron, no shrinking violet himself, cringe. And he could so obsequious Ron would be forced to leave the room to keep from kicking his mentor in the ass.

He was very gentle with Frau Goetz, perhaps because of her recent bereavement, perhaps because he could see that one harsh word might send her screaming down the Boulevard de Ville, perhaps because she was exactly the kind of woman (externally, at least) the old sinner inevitably went for. Ron had long ago given up trying to figure out this part of the old man's technique, and Benedetti had never shown the inclination to teach it.

"It is so good of you to come back to the site of such painful memories," Benedetti said.

"It has been painful," the spirit voice said. "More painful in the time since my husband was . . . killed."

"I want to ask you some questions the police might not have asked you when you were here before. I realize, of course, that I could have had the German authorities ask you the questions at home, but—"

It turned out to be violence.

Gisele Goetz screamed, and her elegant form leaped for the Professor, claws out, raking and tearing like an owl after a mouse. There was blood before Ron could get to her. He was lucky that she didn't try to claw him. But she had eyes (and long red nails) only for Niccolo Benedetti.

Ron got around behind her, grabbed her around the waist, and dragged her backward. She was screaming in German now. Ron reflected that he'd better invest in some Berlitz courses if they were going to take any more of these international cases.

Ron kept backing up until he backed into the chair Frau Goetz had been sitting on. Now he fell into it with the woman on his lap. She was still swinging her arms around, clawing madly at the air. Ron couldn't see much except the fabric in the back of her suit jacket. Carefully (this was one *strong* old lady), Ron let his grip on her waist go, one arm at a time, and regripped her outside her elbows, so that the claws were pinned.

Then she started kicking him in the shins with her heels.

"Mrfmrf," Ron said. He pulled his face away from Frau Goetz's back and tried again. "Janet?"

"What, Ron? The Professor's face is a mess!"

"He'll live. Will you for God's sake do something to help me with this woman? Like call the concierge for manacles or something? I won't be able to walk when she gets through with me."

He heard Janet say, "Hmm, I see what you mean,"

followed by rapid footsteps away. In between shouted curses in German, which seemed to be a very satisfying language to curse in, Ron heard the Professor's muttered curses in Italian, which wasn't bad either. The latter he understood, and Ron was surprised that they were all directed by Niccolo Benedetti at himself. "A clumsy fool" was the mildest thing he called himself.

Ron kept his mouth shut except for the occasional "Ow" when the still-hysterical Frau Goetz connected with a particularly good one against his shin.

Janet was probably not gone longer than fifteen seconds, but it seemed like decades before he heard the returning footsteps.

Ron said, "Well?" just a split second before waves of water crashed down on top of his head and rolled down his arms from his shoulders. It shocked him so much that, for a second, he relaxed his grip on Frau Goetz.

He grabbed her tight again, but he could tell he didn't have to. The woman's body was relaxed now, and he could hear her sputtering as badly as he was.

"Will you be good?" Ron asked. He could see the back of her head move as she nodded.

"You'd better," Janet said. "I've got more water left."

Ron let go. Frau Goetz stood up, and Ron got out from underneath her. Janet handed the widow a towel, and Ron led her to a dry seat.

"I'm sorry I had to do that, Mrs. Goetz," Janet said, "but it's still the best-known practical treatment for hysteria known to science. And there is no doubt you were hysterical."

Gisele Goetz had already sounded like a spirit at a séance and like a Teutonic banshee. Now she unveiled voice number three, soft and pleasant, but achingly sad.

"I suppose now," she said, "you will have me arrested."

Ron and Janet looked at Benedetti. The Professor was holding a red-streaked towel to his cheek. He snorted.

"I am not entirely sure that will be necessary," he said. "But I would like to know the reason for your attack. Are you a madwoman?"

"If I am, it's because of you," she said.

"Madam, I only met you ten minutes ago!"

"Please," she said. Now she sounded disgusted. "I would rather be handed over to the police than listen to such hypocrisy. I returned here to get my claws into whoever was responsible, and now I've done it."

"And so you are satisfied?"

"I am."

"Well, Niccolo Benedetti is not! I have flown six thousand miles to find your husband's killer, and you attack me like an animal! I will know the reason!"

Frau Goetz looked at her hands, clasped demurely in her lap. She ignored the water dripping from her hair.

"Are you truly intent then on going to jail?" Benedetti demanded. For the first time Ron could remember, the old man seemed really *angry*. Ron wondered whether it was the physical injury (even while he reamed the woman out, he kept taking the towel away from his cheek and examining the spreading bloodstain), the injustice of the accusation, or the "If-you-don't-know-I'm-certainly-not-going-to-tell-you" attitude women developed in the Stone Age as revenge for being dragged around by the hair.

More silence.

"It can be arranged, you know. My patience is great, but it is not infinite. *Is* there a reason for your actions here today? Or was it sheer whim?"

Frau Goetz was still looking at her hands.

"Maledizioni," the Professor muttered. "You behaved like an animal here today; one might almost say a she-wolf. Must I add you to my investigations? Travel between Common Market partners is easy and cheap, and a woman who can attack a stranger as you just did might be capable of anything."

Now Gisele Goetz looked up, and the blue eyes were burning. "How dare you?" she said. "Have you no shame at all?"

"I have nothing, madam," Benedetti told her, "except curiosity. I will see it satisfied."

"You," she said. She invested it with all the emotion of one of her German cuss words. "You travel the world exploiting tragedy, until you are God and the victims are forgotten."

Benedetti spoke very quietly. "That is not my intention, madam. Ever. It is because I have my own memories of victims that I do what I do."

Ron shot him a sharp look. Whatever the old man was talking about, it was a story Ron had never heard before.

"Besides," the old man went on, "I believe that what the victims would want most is justice. And I do not boast when I say I have never failed to deliver it."

"Justice!" the woman said. She leaned forward and gripped the cushions of the couch. Ron tensed, thinking that the old man had goaded her back into hysteria. Maybe Benedetti believed in turning the other cheek, but Ron wasn't going to get caught by surprise again. Ron could see that Janet had taken a new grip on her carafe of water.

Whether Gisele Goetz had seen them or not, she subsided a little, and eased back a few inches in her chair.

"Is it justice to blacken the reputation of one of the

finest men who ever lived? With an 'investigation' that can do nothing but start false rumors? Isn't it bad enough my husband had his life stolen from him? Must his good name be taken away, too?"

"How was his good name taken away?" Benedetti asked.

Frau Goetz took a deep breath. "I see you will not be satisfied until my humiliation is complete. Very well. Men from the government have been seeing Hans's colleagues. Some of them two, even three times. They have been asking questions."

"What kind of questions?"

The blue eyes narrowed. "Hateful questions. Embarrassing questions. Questions that leave nasty suspicions in the minds of those who hear them."

"Can you be more specific?"

She shook her head, not saying no, just unable to comprehend what Benedetti could possibly want.

"Questions about Hans. About his ties to the East, to the old regime there. Simply because he was born in Dresden! He made his way to the West with his family, as a teenager."

Hell, Ron thought, even I know that. It had been in the background files Levesque and his staff had put together for them on their arrival. He was pretty sure it had been in the police reports, too.

". . . kept *asking,* and *asking,*" Frau Goetz went on. "*All* his colleagues. Who did he know there? Had he left any relatives in the East? When the wall fell, and the border opened, but before official reunification, was he seen with anyone suspicious? Was he seen with anyone unfamiliar at all?"

"In other words," the Professor said, "was he hiding criminals from the East?"

Frau Goetz gave him a look that could melt lead.

"But that is nonsense," Benedetti said. "East Germany fell quietly. The Communist officials were simply told to go and sin no more. There were no fugitives. No one to aid. Besides, your husband was an astronomer. Of what use could he be?"

"Nonsense," Frau Goetz echoed. This was voice number four, the I'm-about-to-go-nuts voice. "Of course they were nonsense!" she said. "But that won't stop all the people who heard them from wondering if my wonderful husband, who wanted nothing other than to study God's handiwork in the heavens, and help deserving people on earth, was some kind of dirty spy after all. And if you knew they were nonsense, *why did you ask them?*"

"Madam, Niccolo Benedetti endeavors to avoid nonsense at all times. I would scorn to ask such questions."

"You had them asked."

Benedetti looked again at the towel. Ron could see that the bleeding had pretty much stopped, but the old man's cheek was pretty grisly underneath.

The Professor put the towel back in place, took a deep breath, and said, "Aha. Now we come once more to a question that is *not* nonsense, and I beg you to answer it, dear lady. The question is simply this: Why do you think I had those questions asked of your husband's colleagues and friends?"

"Because your so-called investigation is a failure, and you can think of nothing better to do than to blacken the name of a man who was—"

Benedetti had a hand up. "No, madam. Nonononono.

I am sorry. I phrased my question badly. I will try again. Why do you think *I am the one* who caused those questions to be asked?"

"Because they told me so. I—my husband—we had friends in the Ministry of Science. I asked one of them to find out what was going on, soon after I first heard about the questioning. He said the government had nothing to do with it; the investigators were simply doing a favor requested by those in charge of the investigation in France. Then when I was asked to return—"

"You saw your opportunity, and took it," Benedetti said. "I, as an Italian, am perfectly capable of understanding *la vendetta*. When I said *I* was in charge of the investigation, you struck."

Benedetti tried his famous grin, winced, then grinned anyway. "Frau Goetz, I swear to you by all that I hold sacred that I had nothing to do with the blackening of your husband's reputation, and I will devote myself exclusively to clearing it as soon as this investigation is over."

The blue eyes opened wide.

"I further assure you that although your physical vengeance went awry, your actions today have made the ultimate vengeance against whoever is responsible for those ridiculous questions inevitable."

Now Ron's eyes opened wide. "You've got it, Maestro?"

Benedetti shook his head. "Unfortunately, no. I have simply cleared away some underbrush. I regret to say I am no closer to the killer than ever."

Then the Professor did the grin-wince-grin number again. "But perhaps Frau Goetz can help in that regard as well. Madam, we should end this session now. I should have a doctor look at my face, and you, if you'll pardon me, should dry off."

Was that a smile on Gisele Goetz's lips?

"However," Benedetti went on, "if you will be my guest for dinner, I will endeavor to remove any remaining doubts about my innocence, and to ask you the questions I wanted to ask before this unfortunate misunderstanding."

That was when they heard voice number five, a nice, clear woman's voice, with just a twinge of curiosity in it.

"If you like, Professor. Nineteen hours? Seven o'clock?"

Benedetti said that would be fine. Ron shook his head in wonder. The old man was incredible.

20

As Paul Levesque had expected, the international press had been slavering over the latest kill. He was able to return Benedetti safely to the château only because carbine-armed gendarmes held the men with the notebooks and microphones and cameras at bay some half a mile down the road from the château.

This did not prevent, of course, the low-level flyovers by helicopters taking still photos or videos of the "spot where the latest atrocity occurred." He could almost hear them saying it already, then following it with hypocritically sad comments about the fate of OSI and of the baron himself.

Levesque ignored the phones for a few seconds, and allowed himself a fantasy. The fantasy was that the helicopter the baron had purchased from the army still carried its complement of guns. Levesque would have the pilot take him aloft, and he, Levesque, would personally shoot down those vultures who prefer to think of themselves as "journalists."

He smiled sardonically, and thought of what this latest atrocity had done to him. Most of his recent fantasies had been about getting acquainted with Dr. Karin Tebner of the United States.

With a sigh of resignation, Levesque went back to the phones. You could keep the press out of your physical presence, but you couldn't, as the Americans said, stonewall them completely, because then they would *guess*. The guessing would be attributed to "observers" and "informed sources," but it would be guessing all the same. A form of blackmail. The "observers" and the "informed sources" never guessed that the situation was under control, or that an honest effort was being made to correct matters. They always guessed desperation, dark conspiracies, and dirty work.

Levesque supposed one wrote what one was used to in one's own life.

In any case, it did not do to deprive the press of some comment. It wouldn't forestall the guessing, but it *would* ensure that one minuscule percentage of what the public received was a message he wanted to send.

A blanket press release wouldn't do it, either. Everyone wanted to claim an "exclusive interview," even if you told each of them the same things.

Which Levesque was busily doing now.

No, the baron was not a witness to the crime. Yes, the baron was horrified. No, he does not fear for his own life. Yes, Dr. Spaak's loss is a tragic one; he was one of the world's top scientists, or he wouldn't have been invited to participate in the Olympique Scientifique Internationale. No, the baron does *not* regret sponsoring OSI; he regrets that some evil person or persons has ruined it. Every step is being made to safeguard the people of OSI and Mont-St.-Denis; please talk to official police sources for details. Every effort is being made to apprehend the killer; please talk to official police sources for details. The baron has every confidence in the police. The baron also has every confidence in

Professor Niccolo Benedetti, who, you must remember, has been in Mont-St.-Denis less than one week.

There was a lull in the calling. Levesque went to the window for a breath of air and saw the Professor crossing the grounds with Dr. Romanescu.

Another phone rang. Levesque cursed under his breath and went back to his desk. He reached out his hand automatically, before he realized that the light and characteristic buzz had him reaching for the green phone.

The green telephone was the direct line from the offices in Paris. It was never supposed to ring on Sunday, except in cases of dire emergency. In all the years Levesque had worked for the baron, the green phone had always kept the sabbath silently.

Levesque stared at it. He was perfectly willing to concede that he was in fact, in the middle of an emergency, but the emergency was *here,* not in Paris. Had something else happened up there? God forbid.

Levesque's hand was trembling as he picked up the receiver. He managed to keep the tremor out of his voice. "Yes?"

"Monsieur Levesque, this is Jefy, assistant manager of the Paris office. I came in today to clear up the Algerian reports for start of business tomorrow—"

"Very commendable of you," Levesque said. His fear was giving way to irritation.

"—but that is not why I have called, sir. There has been a visitor to the office. He insists on speaking to you personally. He says the ordinary lines are busy."

"They are busy, Jefy. Extremely busy. Right now, they are ringing. That is the squeal of a hungry journalist. Tell your visitor—"

"But Monsieur Levesque, he is—"

Levesque heard heavy footsteps, then a low voice saying, "Give me that." There was an "oof" from someone, probably Jefy, and a new voice came on the line. Levesque recognized it before the second word.

"Levesque, the young genius. I have called to discuss the terms of your employment."

"I am already quite happily employed, Monsieur Caderousse."

"And I am sure you will continue to be. The demise of Monsieur le Baron's business holdings is not your fault. I know how instrumental you have been in helping him to be the nuisance to me he has become.

"Starting tomorrow, when the markets open, I will proceed to maneuver things—in a completely legal manner, I assure you—so that the grand Baron Benac will be forced to sell out to me. I may not get it all—the vultures are circling—but I will get most of it."

"If the others are vultures, does that make you a jackal?"

Caderousse laughed, a deep happy laugh. "If you like. A very, very well fed jackal. My point is this. Among the spoils of victory is your brain. I should like you to employ it in my behalf, rather than against me."

"Never."

"No need to give me your answer now."

"I have given you my answer."

"You may think better of it when you are reduced to managing a few hotels and the vineyard or two I may let your ridiculous employer keep. By the way, may I speak to him?"

"The baron is not available."

Again, the laugh. "Is he trying to pretend his ship is not sinking?"

"The baron is in church," Levesque said.

"I see," Caderousse said. "I can see where he must feel that God has a lot to answer for."

Actually, the baron had stayed after mass to attend a special service, conducted by the bishop, for the souls of the victims, the recovery of young baker Martin (who was still unconscious), and the rapid apprehension of the killer everyone had come to call the Werewolf.

The baron truly believed such things would help. Levesque sincerely wished he could, too. Caderousse would laugh.

"I will speak to you again soon, Monsieur Levesque." He hung up. Levesque did the same.

Damn the man. Damn him. Because he was *right.* If the Werewolf weren't captured immediately—within the next day or so, certainly before the authorities bowed to the inevitable and let the OSI scientists go—the baron would be ruined.

He was too good a man for such a thing to happen to.

But then, by all accounts, the victims had been too good to be murdered.

21

Ion Romanescu spent the afternoon walking quietly around the grounds of the baron's château, visiting the locations of the previous night's remarkable events.

He was, he had been assured, perfectly safe. Not only was it broad daylight, but a full squad of real policemen now stood watch around the grounds. They had, apparently, been requisitioned from the Sûreté by Captain Marx.

It made the Romanian smile to think about it. A squad of French federal officers diverted from their regular duties, simply to protect him. And he did feel safe.

Still, he could be safer.

Retracing Ron Gentry's steps across the lawn toward the site at which Spaak's body had been found, Romanescu found the garden cultivator the young man had mentioned at breakfast that morning. A dangerous thing to leave about. He had found the handle of a hoe, earlier. The brave Mr. Gentry might have broken an ankle if he'd stepped on that.

Romanescu shook his head in disgust. Carelessness. Things like these should not be left about.

Well, he thought, no harm done. Since this was Sunday, the gardeners were not working. Romanescu would simply put the things away himself. He brought the cultivator and the hoe handle over to a faucet on the side of the château. The sun made the water run warm, all the better for getting the dirt and mess off the handles.

"Good afternoon, Doctor!" a voice said.

The Romanian looked up to see Niccolo Benedetti's bulky form looming over him. The Italian had his usual knowing smile on, but it was pulled and twisted out of shape by a bandage on the man's left cheek.

Still staring at the Professor, Romanescu felt his own hand steal to his left cheek, where an identical bandage clung.

"I'm sorry to have startled you," Benedetti said. "I wished to talk to you, and the housekeeper told me you were out wandering the grounds. I came to find you. I hope you do not mind."

Benedetti took a deep breath. "A beautiful day," he said. "On a day like this, it is hard to imagine having an unkind thought. How strange it should follow a night like last night."

Romanescu found his voice. "What has happened to your face?"

Benedetti laughed. "An angry lady," he said. "Not as traumatic as what happened to you, sir, nor as lurid as it sounds. It was a pure misunderstanding on her part. Let no one say Niccolo Benedetti has ever forgotten to be a gentleman."

Then the Professor frowned. The bandage gleamed white in the sun against his nut brown skin. "Why are you working with gardening tools? Doesn't the baron have a large enough staff?"

Suddenly, Romanescu felt guilty. The ability to make others feel guilty was a decided asset in an inquisitor. Such an ability had taken men far—Benedetti, had he desired, could have been an important man in the Romanian secret police. Romanescu's countrymen, even those who should be relatively immune, were conditioned to respond to it, as he was doing now. He vowed to himself not to show it.

"Tools left around," he said. "You recall your assistant mentioning he almost stepped on a cultivator. I've found these; I thought I'd put them away before anyone got hurt."

"Va bène," Benedetti said. "I will walk with you."

They started across the lawn. Suddenly, Romanescu let loose with a little burst of laughter.

"You know, Professor," he said. "We are wasting this. We should walk together in Paris, where all the trends are set. We might be able to start a fashion."

Benedetti laughed and nodded. "The bandaged cheek look! We could sell designer bandages."

"Become rich. Retire to America."

"I already live in America. But I shall never retire. I have too much work to do."

Romanescu sighed. "I lived for years longing for a chance to do my proper work, and once that opportunity came, I found that the field had passed me by." He shook his head. "I can't call myself an astronomer any more—indeed, if I ever could. So I *am* retired, whether I wish to be or not."

He turned eagerly to the Professor. "But I think I should like to come to America. I would prefer not to return to Romania—too many memories."

"America would be glad to welcome you, I am sure," Benedetti said.

"A penniless old man with no skill? How do you put it in capitalist countries? No *marketable* skill? I would need help I have no right to ask for."

"I have done a favor or two, over the years . . ." Benedetti began.

"You would help me? Then I renounce my fears. With the great Niccolo Benedetti on my side, how can I fail?"

"That can wait," Benedetti said, suddenly brusque. It was as if he was disciplining himself. He liked to hear people say "the great Niccolo Benedetti" too much to show it.

"Right now," Benedetti went on, "I want to ask you about last night."

Romanescu made a slight bow. "Anything I can do to help."

"Va bène. You were asleep with the windows open last night, then, is that correct?"

"Yes. I talked myself into bravery."

"Did you hear anything before Ron Gentry woke you?"

Romanescu shrugged. "I am a very sound sleeper. In a police state one learns to ignore much in order to sleep. After he woke me, I heard many things. Alarms, sirens, shoutings, and screamings—"

"Yes, Doctor, we all heard too much of that. Did you go to the window?"

"Yes, I did. Even before I opened the door. I wanted to see what was going on. I had a fine view of the fence, as you know. Mr. Gentry looked out a few seconds later."

"Did you look away from the fence at all?"

"Of course, I must have. An astronomer can stare for hours only at the stars."

"You saw no one on the lawn, then."

"Only your assistant. He went out that same window. A very brave young man."

"He is, indeed," Benedetti said. "Sometimes too brave

to suit either his wife or me. Did you hear anything other than what you have already described?"

Romanescu stuck his tongue out the side of his mouth and thought. "No. No, nothing."

"And you might not have recognized anything if you did hear it," Benedetti mumbled. "One thing a man might recognize in the midst of chaos is his own name. Did you hear anyone mention your name?"

"No, I heard nothing like that."

They had reached the shed. It was latched, but not locked. Romanescu opened the door, quickly put the cultivator and the hoe back in their appointed places in the crowded tool racks that lined the walls, then closed up.

As they walked back toward the house, the Professor seemed lost in thought. Romanescu let it go on for a few seconds, then touched the Italian on the arm and said, "May I, er, ask the purpose of your questions, Professor?"

"I dislike false assumptions," Benedetti said.

"Yes?"

"And everyone, even my own assistants, seems to believe that whatever went on here last night was part of an abortive attempt to get to you, as the only witness to the first attack. The guards' being brought here shows that the official police credit that possibility."

"I am glad," Romanescu said distinctly, "that they are here to watch over me."

Benedetti once again crinkled his bandage with a smile. "I would not have them go away," he said. "I could be wrong. But this does seem to conflict with your werewolf theory. I have never heard of a werewolf in legend or fiction who marked out victims beforehand, or who worried about witnesses."

"You embarrass me, Professor," Romanescu admitted.
"I had been . . . Well, perhaps I can make you understand my state of mind. After years of tension in my homeland, I was at last free to come here. I would have no
worries; it would be like heaven. Then a great man is murdered virtually around the corner from me; I am myself
attacked. A month of pain and anxiety. Then, with the next
full moon, it happens again. I snapped. I lived for a time in
the fairy tales my mother told my brother and me to
frighten us. I am back in reality, now."

Romanescu raised a hand. "That is not to say, however, that I am not still afraid. You implied the idea of the
killer trying to get me is a *false* assumption. Why?"

"What was Dr. Spaak doing here? More specifically,
why was he in this vicinity yet outside the fence? If the—
I'll call him the Werewolf for want of a better name—if the
Werewolf wanted to kill you, why didn't he at least *try* to
get in and do something about you? He could not have
known the baker would come by and discover the body so
soon."

"There was the alarm fence," Romanescu pointed out.

"That doesn't matter," Benedetti said. "Either he
knew about the alarm fence, or he didn't. Either he had a
plan to circumvent the alarm, or he didn't care." Benedetti
shrugged. "Ah, well, perhaps the baker's setting off the
alarm frightened him away. In any case, it will be instructive to question the young man. Why didn't the Werewolf
attack him, too, as you were attacked?"

"No, my friend, I hold to my belief that the Werewolf
is doing precisely what he intends to do. And I don't believe
he intends to kill you."

"He made a good try," Romanescu said.

Benedetti touched his own cheek. "I don't know about

that. What we have experienced is disquieting to see and painful to experience, but when all is said and done, it is fairly minor damage. A slender woman of late middle age can inflict it. Compare that with the torn-out throats of de Blois and Spaak, the immolation of Goetz's mangled body. I believe our killer could have killed you then, if he'd intended to."

Benedetti scratched his chin. "Now, if I could only figure out *why* you were spared, perhaps I could lay hands on the killer."

The Professor mused for a moment, then shook himself and said, "I've quite enjoyed our walk together. I won't be joining the rest of you for dinner. Take care, Doctor, and don't worry." He ambled toward the house with an effortless, ground-eating stride.

Romanescu stood and watched him go. Somehow, he was not comforted.

22

The baron knelt and listened in the darkness of the cathedral, and for a moment, indulged himself in a feeling of despair and guilt, almost letting himself believe that God had sent the Werewolf to punish him for the pride he had taken in the Olympique Scientifique Internationale. The fear, the suspicion, the failure, the threat of the loss of all his holdings as his public stature waned, all seemed to have been sent to teach him humility.

But this, Pierre Benac realized almost too late, this itself was pride, a deadly snare of the devil's. To think that a good God would waste innocent lives and scar the psyches of thousands of people simply to teach one insignificant man a lesson was a fearful sin, and the baron repented of it as soon as it had been committed.

The baron bowed his head. He realized that the answer to this was not as simple, and as (secretly) gratifying as all that. OSI had been the victim of evil, nasty, skulking, everyday evil, the sort of evil men had it in their power to stop.

And so, the baron prayed for enlightenment to come. Not necessarily to him personally, whose brain had reeled helplessly since this had all begun, but to *someone*. And soon.

Janet had gone to the hospital in order to use the computer to access worldwide case files. She hadn't even asked first—she'd gotten used to anything the baron was connected with being a first-class job.

That was the case here. If anything in anybody's medical computer anywhere could help someone who took sick or got injured on the slopes of Mont-St.-Denis, the folks here at the hospital would have access to it. Whether they'd know what to do with it was another thing.

Janet, for instance, had filled half a notebook, but she'd be damned if she knew if it would do the investigation the slightest bit of good.

She looked at her watch. Still several hours before she had to meet Ron and get picked up to go back to the château. As long as she was here, she decided, she might as well go up and see the poor boy who'd been hit on the head last night.

She'd picked a good time. Prefect Diderot and several of his men were rushing down the hallway toward the room as Janet got off the coffinlike, doorless European elevator.

Diderot stopped and glared at her. "Did the Professor send you? How did he know?"

"How did he know what?" Janet demanded.

"That young Martin had awakened. I was down the hall, and I just heard it myself."

"Coincidence," she said. "Honestly. I just thought I'd come up and visit."

Captain Marx caught up with them. "And we are simply supposed to believe that?" he sneered.

All her life, Janet had been shy. She'd had to train

herself not to defer automatically to anyone who acted sure of himself. She used to tell herself it probably would have been easier to train herself to climb Mount Everest naked.

Even now, in the face of Marx's attack, part of her cringed, didn't want to offend, didn't want to make trouble. That was the part that had to be suppressed.

"I don't really care, Captain," she said, "what you believe." She pulled up out of her habitual slouch and glared down at him from her full five-foot-eleven-inch height.

She turned a milder version of the glare on Diderot. "The fact is, this has happened, and I am here. I'll be there while you question him, as Professor Benedetti's representative."

Marx snorted. "Think again, Mademoiselle."

"Maybe it would be better for you, Captain, to *begin* to think. The Professor was promised, as a condition of joining this investigation, the *full* cooperation of the authorities."

"Provided he did not interfere."

"I won't interfere."

"Your very presence in that room would be interference."

Janet adjusted her glasses and raised one eyebrow. "Then there's nothing more to say," she said.

"At last one of you Americans shows some sense."

"Nothing more to say to *you,* that is. I'm sure the hundreds of reporters who have been badgering the Professor would love a statement saying Niccolo Benedetti has withdrawn from the case because Captain Samuel Marx of the Sûreté in Paris has broken his word about cooperating with him."

"He wouldn't dare."

Diderot chuckled. "Why would he not, you fool?

What harm would it do to have Dr. Higgins there? She is, after all, a psychologist. Perhaps she can offer insights into young Martin's answers."

Marx blew out air. "Very well," he said. "Come if you must." The captain was trying to maintain his air of sophisticated disgust, but Janet could see that the man was immensely relieved to have been offered a way out.

In any case, the whole argument had been a waste of effort, because young Martin had nothing to say except that he'd found the body, received a dangerous shock, then had been waylaid by two guns-wielding lunatics (against whom he intended to press charges), and had defended himself the best way he could, until a third cowardly attacker left him open for the blow that even now made his head feel like the inside of his father's hottest oven.

Janet learned from further questions that Martin wasn't even a serious suspect—there was no blood on his knife, or on him, and nothing else outside the fence that could have inflicted Spaak's wound. The policemen filled the air with routine questions until the doctor called a halt. "A fractured skull is a serious thing, you must remember," he said.

"Well," Marx said once they were back in the hallway. "Long live cooperation. Do you have any insights for us?"

"Nothing except that he's angry and scared and almost certainly innocent."

"I envy him," Marx said. "To be certainly innocent of anything in this day and age is a remarkable achievement."

He lit a cigarette. "The prefect and I are now going to discuss what to make of the testimony of this young man who saw or heard nothing except the corpse, and who thought of nothing but the corpse. Would it please you to join us?"

"Why are you so offensive? Is it natural, or do you try to cultivate it for some reason?"

"Offensive? I said *please,* did I not?"

"Never mind," Janet said, tired of the bickering and very tired of Captain Marx. "Go have your meeting. I'll skip it."

"Are you sure? I would hate to show a lack of cooperation."

It was too good an opportunity for Janet to pass up. "You've shown a lot of improvement. I'll make it a point to tell the Professor."

Marx stared for a long moment, then walked away. He wasn't quite snarling.

As Janet was handing in her visitor's badge at the main desk of the hospital, someone grabbed her arm. Anger drowned out shyness, and she whirled around, ready to give Captain Marx or one of his minions a piece of her mind.

Instead, she found herself looking at the freckled face of Dr. Karin Tebner.

"Dr. Higgins?" the astronomer said. "May I talk to you for a moment?"

"Of course," Janet said. "Here?"

Dr. Tebner took a quick glance at the elevator. "No. Not here. Let's take a walk."

"Good idea," Janet said. "Let's do that."

They strolled out of the lobby and down the Boulevard de Ville.

"Dr. Higgins—" Dr. Tebner began.

It wasn't like Janet to interrupt (it wasn't very good tactics for a shrink, come to that), but there was something about the other woman that she liked.

"Look," Janet said. "If we go back and forth with 'Dr.

Higgins' and 'Dr. Tebner,' we're going to sound like a symposium. If you'll be Karin, I'll be Janet, okay?"

"If I'll be Karin," Karin echoed. "God, I'd like to do that for a weekend or two. Sam calls me Karin because I've told him to, but he stumbles over it every time."

"Sam? Oh, Captain Marx. You came to the hospital with him?"

"We were having lunch."

"Won't he be mad that you've walked out on him?"

"I don't think so."

"He's been spending a lot of time with you, from what I've heard."

Karin rolled her eyes. "My God," she said.

"Do you mean, 'My God, people have heard,' or 'My God, a *lot* of time?' "

"Both. You mean people think I'm having a *romance* with him or something?"

"Well, he seems devoted to you. Don't you like him?"

"Oh, I like him all right. He's polite and attentive. He can even be charming when he wants to be. Are you all right?"

Janet had choked on the thought that she was talking about the same Captain Marx. "Yes," she coughed. "Yes, I'm fine. Just swallowed wrong."

"But there's nothing *personal* in it," Karin went on. "I think I'm just as glad to have it that way."

"Why's that?"

"Because he can be scary, too. He says he's spending all this time with me because he thinks I know something I don't realize I know and that I might be in danger."

"Hardly romantic."

Karin was emphatic. "Like I said, there's nothing romantic about it. I hang around with him for the same reasons. I mean, he's a cop on this case, he must know *something.*"

A few blocks from the hospital, they paused at the corner to let the slow Sunday traffic go by, then crossed to the stretch of the boulevard down which Karin had run the morning she'd found the body. The astronomer froze in her tracks for a few seconds, then shook herself and walked on.

"Sorry," Karin said, "I always shudder when I think about it."

"Don't think about it right now. There's something you wanted to ask me, isn't there? I mean, you didn't approach me just to tell me about your relationship with Captain Marx, did you?"

Karin laughed. "Such as it is. No, I didn't. I wanted to ask you—well, no offense—"

"It's okay. It's impossible to offend a psychologist."

"It is?"

Now Janet laughed. "No, it's only supposed to be. But you're not a patient, anyway. Don't let me treat you like one. It's a bad habit we can get into."

"Astronomers get stiff necks." Karin was suddenly serious. "Janet, what happened to Dr. Spaak?"

Janet took a deep breath. "About the same thing that happened to the others."

"Did you see him?"

"No. But for my sins, I'll have to look at the pictures later."

"Uhhh. Why?"

"Actually, I'll have to look at all the pictures. I have to see if these things match the pathology of lycanthropism."

"You mean people who think they're werewolves?"

"Yeah. I've been at the hospital, boning up."

Janet stopped herself just in time from sharing all the interesting stuff she'd found out.

"But, Karin, I don't think you've asked me the question you want to ask yet."

"No, I haven't," she said, and they walked on for awhile until they came to the Place du Science, with its now-extinguished torch covered in black cloth.

"It was so horrible!" Karin said. "I haven't been able to convey to anybody how awful it was. The smell, and the feel, and the realization that someone had held him up there until he—until he'd burned enough to—to stick."

"That's enough of that," Janet said. "Next walk I'll take with you will be along the back streets. This question of yours must be really something, if you'd rather talk about this stuff."

"It's not all *that* bad," Karin said. Still, she hesitated.

Janet made her voice mock-gruff. "Out with it, Dr. Tebner!"

"All right. Do you think Dr. Spaak was killed because he talked to you?"

"Actually, he talked to my husband."

Karin waved a flat palm across the air, as though erasing a slate.

"No," she said, "I mean, do you think he was killed for trying to organize the scientists in an effort to find the Werewolf?"

Janet noted with greater than academic interest that there were no audible quotes around the name of the killer any more.

She answered the question. "I don't know. I just don't know."

"Do you think it's possible?"

Such were the dynamics of the team she formed with

the Professor and Ron that Janet Higgins was rarely the one who got asked that question. She didn't quite know what to do with it.

"Me?" she said. "Personally? Yes, I do. Serial killers have enormous, unbridled egos. They can come to resent anyone getting as much publicity from their crimes as they do themselves. Sometimes—"

"Well, don't stop *now.*"

Janet saw the smile of exaggerated exasperation on Karin's face, and it occurred to her that the two of them had begun acting as if they'd been friends for years. Should she be suspicious of that kind of instinct, or should she run with it?

She decided to run with it.

"Sometimes—frequently—a serial killer will go out of his way to involve himself with the case. Get close to the investigators somehow, or turn up as a 'key witness.' "

There was a moment's silence. At last Karin said, "Like me, you mean?"

"What?" Janet felt herself blushing. "Nonono," she said, "I didn't mean you." A voice somewhere inside her asked *why not?* but she forced it to go away.

"Listen," she said, "what you need is a change of scene."

"Right," Karin said. "Back to New Mexico. It's boring and empty, but at least nobody gets killed. I can be packed in half an hour."

"Maybe what I should have said is a change of company. Why don't you come back to the château with me and join us for dinner tonight?"

"I couldn't."

"Why not? The baron told us specifically to use any

and all of his resources if it will help the investigation. Keeping you sane will help."

"Will I have to see where Dr. Spaak—"

Janet shook her head. "No, not even close. Come on, Ron and I will be lonely. The Professor is going out, and the baron, from what I understand, is going into seclusion. Dr. Romanescu announced at breakfast he would eat in his room. That leaves it up to us, and we're planning to keep it informal. You won't even have to change."

"Well . . ."

"I'll tell you one thing," Janet said. "We haven't had much satisfaction out of this trip so far, but the food the baron's chef whips up is *great*. Besides, you'll give Marx something to worry about for a change."

Karin laughed. "Okay," she said. "You talked me into it. But I would like to go back to my place and change, anyway. I brought a dress with me; this looks like the best excuse I'll have to wear it."

23

The driver got out of the car and opened the front door of the château for them. Karin saw Janet nod her thanks as she walked in.

"Did you grow up rich or something?" Karin asked.

"Nothing special. My dad's a dentist. Why?"

"You handled all that so well. I always feel weird around servants."

"Me, too," Janet said. "Or, I used to. The Good Life is remarkably easy to get used to."

A young man Karin recognized as Janet's husband was bent over a telephone on a small table in the middle of the vast room that must be the Great Hall. He held a list in his hand.

". . . No, Paul, I mean it. The Professor would appreciate it if you had the baron dressed and down here ready to go in—" He looked at his watch. "My God, in seven minutes. No, I am *not* presuming to tell my host what to do. I am presuming to tell my host that the man he sent across the ocean for is about to deliver the goods, and that my host might want to be there when the truck pulls up."

Ron listened for a few moments, bouncing his head impatiently. "Not in so many words," Ron said. "But I know the signs. They wouldn't mean anything to you. Okay, he finished a painting, and he's letting something interfere with a date." More head-bobbing. "Just do the best you can, then."

Janet seemed to forget Karin was here. She sprinted across the hall to her husband and grabbed his arm just as he put down the phone. "Ron!" she said. "He finished a painting? An abstract?"

"Hi, honey," he said, and gave his wife a quick kiss. Karin saw that with long practice, they had managed to develop a way to do that without clicking glasses.

"Yeah, he finished one. A great one. Why don't you go take a look at it? I've still got people to track down."

Janet took the list from him and scanned it. "You can scratch Karin Tebner," she said.

"No, I can't! The old man was emphatic. Said she had a right to be in on the close, too. Same with Romanescu. Right here under this roof, but he was the hardest of all. Still scared. I had to practically promise him American citizenship to get him to come along."

"Karin Tebner is here. I brought her with me."

Ron raised his brows. "I'm impressed. ESP?"

"Dumb luck. I invited her for dinner."

"Maybe later. Right now, the Professor's idea, as I understand it, is to drive around town and pick everybody up in one car, like the end of *The Huckleberry Hound Show.* Maybe two cars—he's got a lot of people here."

A sudden thought lit up the detective's face. "Dr. Tebner," he called out. "Why don't you come a little closer so we don't have to shout."

Karin complied.

"Hi," he said. "Nice to meet you at last. I assume you've heard what we've been saying."

"Yes. Are you really saying Professor Benedetti has figured out who's committed these murders?"

"*He* sure thinks so. I've never seen him get like this and be wrong yet."

"I've never seen him get like this at all," Janet put in. "What happened?"

Ron shrugged. "I brought him the police reports. They clinch it that the baker boy is off the hook, by the way. Lab makes it certain. The rest of it is just so much scrap paper."

Janet interrupted to tell him that young Martin had awakened and looked as if he was going to be fine.

For some reason, Janet's husband looked relieved, as though he'd been the one who hit the boy on the head. There was a lot going on here Karin didn't understand.

"Anyway," Ron Gentry went on, "I don't know what happened. I brought him the pile from last night, he looked through it, then went off into the bathroom to shave.

"He told me to wait for him, so I did. A few seconds later, I hear the water running, I hear a tearing noise, and I hear a scream."

"A scream?" Janet sounded incredulous. "From the *Professor?* I can't believe it, either."

"Neither did I. I was afraid he'd pulled his bandage off too fast and set himself bleeding again, or that he'd slipped with that damn deadly cutthroat razor he insists on shaving with and sliced his scabs off.

"It turned out not to be a scream; it turned out to be a high-volume '*Aha!*' He rushed from the bathroom to the easel, whipped the cover off the current painting, said 'Buon Iddìo, now I know what I was trying to tell myself!' and signed the painting. Then he gave me this shopping list of people to get together and things to arrange. Which I am still trying to do. Dr. Tebner!"

Karin jumped.

"I'm delighted you're here, not only because that Italian madman wants you to be, but because *I* want to ask you a question. From a few words the old man let slip, I suspect he may be intending for this particular fire drill to wind up at the observatory. Who's the best person to contact to assure we can be let in?"

"That's no problem," Karin said. "I've got a key. We've all got keys. Dr. Romanescu could have let you in, I suppose."

"I didn't think to ask him. Thank you, that's wonderful. Now I've got to get back to the phone. Why don't you go along with my wife, and let her try to explain to you the way a genius's mind works?"

Janet saw Karin Tebner's face looking expectantly at her as they climbed the stairs, and she began to appreciate how Ron felt on those occasions when the Professor announced that his associate was now going to explain one aspect of the case or another.

"He paints," Janet said. "All during a case, he paints at a furious pace. Acrylics. The closer he gets to a solution, the more abstract the canvas gets. He says he lets his subconscious mind paint what it sees. If you can understand the last canvas, you can usually figure out what he's figured out."

"And that's it?" Karin asked. "That's how he's caught all these murderers?"

"Oh, Lord, no," Janet said. "That's just all I'm able to explain. You'll have to see him in action to appreciate the rest."

"This is kind of exciting," Karin said.

Janet looked at her and said, "Mmmm. I'm going to have to keep you away from my husband, I can see that."

"Why?"

"Because he says there's not one woman in ten thousand who'll admit that, and that's one of the reasons he loves me. And now, here you are, and now I'm not one in ten thousand any more."

"I've only seen you together for a total of about three minutes, after the meeting in the cathedral and just now downstairs, and I don't think you have anything to worry about. You're obviously crazy about each other."

"I know," Janet said. "It's a continuing pleasant surprise."

Janet walked up to the Professor's door and knocked. "Professor, it's me, Janet. Ron sent me to see the painting."

"Aspetta, cara," the Professor said from the other side of the door. "Wait just a moment, please. Have you spoken to your husband?"

"Just for a second. I ran into Dr. Tebner. She's out here in the hall with me."

"Excellent, excellent!" The door opened between the first and second excellent. "Please come in, ladies. Dr. Tebner, I am charmed to meet you." He kissed her hand. Karin blushed, just as Janet had the first time he'd done it to her.

Professor Benedetti looked in the mirror and gave one last tug to his bow tie. He smelled faintly of witch hazel. He had gotten his shave, after all—a fresh bandage gleamed on his cheek.

"Is this it, Professor?" Janet asked.

"It is, *cara*. I have staked our reputations on it. So please, tell me all you have seen and heard and done since last we were together, just in case there is a little fact that remains to be accounted for."

Janet wasn't as good at reporting as Ron was, but then he got a lot more practice. She tried especially hard because an outsider was listening.

When she finished, the Professor grinned at her and said, "Excellent. Why did you decide to make this study of lycanthropy?"

"I've been meaning to all the time, but things have been so hectic since we got here, it's the first time I had the chance."

"Yes, but why?"

"All we've heard since we got started on this was werewolf, werewolf. Because of the full moon, I suppose. But it's also true that each murder has been more savage, more wolflike. Or *were*wolflike, I should say. Real wolves hunt in packs, and usually strangle their victims as much as maim them."

Benedetti shook his head. "It is tragic I did not have a chance to train you when you were younger. You have placed a finger on one of the key aspects of the case."

He turned to Karin. "And you, Dr. Tebner, your instincts are good as well. I should have made time to interview you on that first day. For you have been asking an important question: *Why was Dr. Goetz burned?*

"Indeed, I owe my entire solution, it seems, to women, since it was Frau Goetz who provided me with the clue I should have understood the day of our arrival."

"What clue is that, Professor?" Janet asked.

"I didn't tell your husband, neither will I tell you. You have both seen it. I cannot blame you; I failed to notice its significance, too, as did the prefect."

"And Captain Marx," Karin said. "I've been in his

company a lot lately, and all he talked about was 'not one single clue.' I'm not saying he would have mentioned a clue if there was one, but he wouldn't have said what he did, either."

"Ah, yes, Captain Marx." There was a reddish gleam of glee in the Professor's grin now. "We must not expect too much in the way of spotting clues from the captain. I now know quite a bit about Captain Marx. I too, have been making telephone calls."

"He was on Ron's list of people to find," Janet said.

"Oh, yes. I wouldn't dream of doing this without our Alsatian friend. We will find his presence indispensible."

"And now, ladies," said the Professor, offering an arm to each, "shall we go downstairs and see how Ronald is faring?"

24

"Wait a minute!" Janet said. She was surprised to hear herself give what was in effect an order to the great Niccolo Benedetti—even Ron didn't try that sort of thing much—but she didn't want to look like a wimp in front of the visitor either.

Benedetti seemed amused. "Of course, of course. We have promised our visitor a look at my work. I apologize for letting it slip my mind. Wait a moment, please."

The Professor left the room, returning just a few seconds later with a burlap-covered rectangle. He put it on a chair.

"Please remember, Dr. Tebner," he said, "not to judge too harshly. I am but an amateur, and I paint for reasons other than those of aesthetics."

Then the old man proved himself a liar by whipping the burlap off the canvas with the air of a magician showing you that he's made the tiger disappear.

Janet looked at it. As Ron had said, it was one of his best. At first, all she could notice was the striking design, three rough overlapping ovals, with modifications. The oval in the foreground was black, a little longer than the others, with two large points on the top, and some small jagged ones projecting from the bottom. This overlapped a white oval, smudged here and there with red. Behind both was a blood red oval, with the shades ranging from almost-orange to almost-purple. All this was set against a purplish, light gray background that suggested torn newsprint.

At second glance, Janet could see that the ovals were faces—those pointed projections on the black one could be the ears and teeth of a stylized wolf. The red smudges on the white oval could represent the victims. Janet had no idea what the red oval could mean, but as she stared at it, the pattern of the subtle color differences suggested an evil, grinning face. The devil? Only Benedetti could say.

Right now, he only said, "Comment, Dr. Tebner?"

"It's amazing, Professor," Karin said. She was still staring at it. "I don't think I'll ever forget it. But I wouldn't want to live with it."

Benedetti's chuckle was not without warmth. "You would not welcome it as a housewarming present, then?"

Karin shook her head. "Not even if I had a house," she said. She still hadn't stopped looking at it. "I couldn't sit in front of that and watch TV or eat Grape-Nuts or do any of the stuff I ordinarily do. I don't know if I'm making any sense at all. . . ."

Janet, who had a houseful of paintings like this, all banished to rooms into which she never went, thought she was not only making sense, but expressing it better than she herself ever could.

"You're doing fine," Janet said.

"This painting *attacks* me," Karin said. "Powerfully. It fills my head with strange ideas, and I can't even recognize what they are. I hope you're not offended, Professor."

"Far from it, Doctor. You see, I paint the picture to get those same ideas—which, at the the time, Niccolo Benedetti *also* fails to understand—*out* of my poor old head." He tapped his temple. "Then, when they're out where I can see them, they sometimes help me to understand the truth once I stumble over it."

"And this has done that?"

"It has indeed. It has helped make tangible the motives for the crime."

"Which was?"

The Professor sighed. "Hans Goetz was killed because he was too good; Captain de Blois because he was inconvenient; Dr. Spaak because he *was* convenient."

Karin screwed up her face and said, "Huh?" Janet wanted to hug her.

"It will become, I hope, apparent soon enough. If you desire to see the painting for a longer time, I suggest you leave that until we return here later. Now, I really think we should go downstairs."

Levesque was standing in the main hall, dressed to go out. Anger had made him tight-lipped, except when he had to speak to soothe the baron, who was not a man who tended toward serenity at the best of times.

"Yes, Monsieur le Baron, I'm sure they know what they're talking about. Remember, Professor Benedetti is the best in the world. Remember also your principle—hire the best, then let them work. If results are at hand, we must be patient, no?"

Levesque said all that in the most soothing tones he could muster, then proceeded to argue with himself. What kind of business is this Gentry trying to pull? He forces me to disturb a miserable old man and hustle him down to the Great Hall. When we have arrived, he looks at us, says "Good," consults a list, says "Wait here," and disappears.

And this Benedetti may be the best in the world, but

what has he really done except eat the baron's food, make philosophical pronouncements, and look on as murder came practically to the baron's doorstep? "Hire the best and let them work," yes. But sooner or later one must notice that even the best has failed, and—

Here came the old man now, down the main stairs as if *he* were the baron, making an entrance. He had Gentry's wife with him and—who else was that?

Bon dieu, it was Karin Tebner. In a dress. Smiling at him.

Levesque scarcely heard as Janet performed the introductions; he was enjoying the lightly-freckled smile of the American astronomer. He had hoped someday she would smile at him, and now here it was, when he needed it most.

Dr. Tebner was speaking to the baron. ". . . want you to know that OSI was a wonderful and noble idea, and no matter what's happened, I'll always be proud to have been chosen for it."

The baron patted her hand and smiled. His eyes were just a little damp. The baron had needed to hear something like that. Levesque had suspected that Karin Tebner would be like that—a woman who seemed to have an instinct for doing the little things a man needed.

"And you, M. Levesque. After all your work. I never got a chance to thank you for the way you made us all feel at home at orientation."

"Uh, why don't you call me Paul?"

Janet Higgins smiled a "bless you, my children" smile. She had it in the back of her mind someday to write a paper on the urge to matchmake, but she realized it would be difficult for her to maintain the necessary scientific detachment.

It would be like asking Attila the Hun to do a paper on aggression.

Right now, it was enough to see Karin telling Paul to call her Karin, and to see the shy smiles flying between them. It might have seemed an odd time to an outsider, but then, she'd met Ron in the middle of a murder investigation, and that had worked out fine.

Dr. Romanescu came downstairs to join them. He had a fearful look on his face. Shame, Janet thought. He'd been making progress, too. She wished Ron were here now to help her keep an eye on him.

And that led her to wonder where the heck he was. She'd just assumed he was off fetching Romanescu.

She asked the Professor where her husband was.

"In the kitchen, I suspect," the old man said. "Either that or the vegetable pantry."

Ron had just finished closing the bag when Janet joined him in the kitchen.

"What's in the bag?" she asked.

"Apples, mostly. The biggest ones I could find. Unfortunately, none of the ones here are very big, even the baking apples."

"Apples."

"The Professor specified apples."

"In case he gets hungry or something? Ron, what is this?"

"Darling, your guess is as good as mine. He said I should definitely get some apples, enough for everybody, but that I should look around for something better."

"Better for what?"

"He didn't say. I asked him, and he said, I had a mind,

and he had trained it, and I should know. He did tell me that cabbage was the right size but the wrong texture, the skin of a melon was too thick, and that potatoes would do if I couldn't find the apples. Mean anything to you?"

Janet was totally bewildered. "Do you think he's finally lost his mind?"

"You're the shrink, my dear. What do you think?"

"Of course I don't think so. But apples, potatoes, cabbages, melons—what does that have to do with anything?"

Ron shrugged. "Crazy crimes, crazy solution. Let's just trust the old man."

25

Janet sat in the cable car and looked out across the sky at the lopsided but still impressive moon that rose over the Republic of France. They made quite a carful, once they were gathered all together.

Diderot and Marx stood by the door of the cable car, as though preventing one of these dangerous characters from making a break through the door, some hundreds of feet above a particularly unsoft-looking Alpine valley. The prefect seemed bland, a man doing his job. Marx, as usual, scowled. Janet tried to see if the scowl deepened when the captain's gaze passed over Karin Tebner and Paul Levesque, who sat whispering together in a corner of the car.

The baron sat near them, looking distracted. He looked, in fact, well on his way to disassociating. Janet asked him a question every now and then to keep him in the here and now.

She did the same for Romanescu, who sat on the other side of her. If the Romanian had made a list of all the places in the world in the order he'd enjoy being there, Janet suspected the observatory would be third from the bottom, ahead of back in Romania and back in the clutches of the Werewolf.

Gisele Goetz sat on the other side of Romanescu. She

had quickly taken in the fact that her quiet dinner/question session with Professor Benedetti had turned into what the old man hoped would be a surprise party for the killer, and had come along without a word.

She was still silent, looking out the window, sometimes biting her lower lip, as though to keep some emotion in check. Memories of making this trip with her husband, Janet thought. Or hope that Benedetti really had it.

Ron and the Professor sat in the far corner of the car, not saying much, just exchanging knowing looks. Janet undoubtedly would have been welcome to join them, but she was mad at her husband.

Janet had brought Ron and his bag of fruit back to the Great Hall of the baron's château just as the police had arrived.

Diderot was tense, but expectant. He asked the Professor what he was planning.

"That will become clear as the evening unfolds."

"Professor, please—"

"Truly, Monsieur le Préfect, I am not making mysteries for the sport of it."

Janet looked at her husband, who was heroically repressing either a snort or a sardonic laugh. The effort gave his face a pained look.

"But," the old man continued, "you are going to hear a complex and bizarre story this evening, and perhaps see a demonstration. I want you to experience it at the same time these people do, and in the proper setting, in order that you feel the full effect. You, after all, will make the arrest, and it is you who shall have to present the case to those above you."

"Right," Marx snarled. The inevitable cigarette bounced on his lip. "I never thought I'd hear you concede the fact, Professor. *We* are the officials here. We have the responsibility for making the arrest. No pledges of official cooperation can change that fact."

"We, Monsieur Marx?" the Professor asked blandly.

"Oui, vraiment," Marx said.

"Forgive me," Benedetti told him. "I was not speaking French. I was questioning, *monsieur,* your pronoun in English."

Ron leaned over and whispered to Janet. "Is that some kind of insult or something?"

"What do you mean?"

"The Professor has gone out of his way twice in fifteen seconds not to call Marx 'Captain.' Is that some kind of French insult or something?"

Janet shook her head; it wasn't that she knew of.

"Furthermore, I have no intention of impinging on the prefect's authority. Monsieur le Préfect, if you prefer that I refrain from proceeding with my demonstration, simply say so."

Diderot looked at Benedetti, then Marx, then back to Benedetti. "I am most eager," he said at last, "to witness your demonstration, Professor."

"Va bène," Benedetti said. "Your trust in me is an honor. I will do my best to be worthy of it. You will not regret this."

Benedetti took a deep breath, looked around to see everyone gathered, and said, "Well, then, are we all ready to go?"

Actually, by this time, they were ready to bust down the door to get the show on the road. There was a chorus of yeses in two languages.

But Benedetti said, "No."

Everyone from the baron on down looked as if they

could gladly lynch the Professor, and Janet wasn't devoid of that impulse either.

Benedetti was serene. "Ronald, would you please go to my room and get my ointment, bandages, and tape?"

Ron's brow furrowed. "Bandages?"

"That is correct. I have a feeling I might need a change of dressing before the night is over. In fact, I am virtually certain."

Benedetti looked hard at Ron, a look that blended sternness with expectation. It was exactly the look Janet used to give the bright student from whom she was expecting the clever answer. She knew then that Benedetti hadn't forgotten anything. This whole bandage business had been staged to give Ron one more chance to make the breakthrough on his own.

And as Janet watched, damned if he didn't make it.

Ron's lips snapped shut and his eyes opened wide behind his glasses. Then he opened his mouth and breathed like a little boy, *"Apples!"*

Benedetti just looked wise. "I will hold the bag of apples. Just go get the bandages, please."

And Ron was off. He was so charged by whatever it was he'd seen that linked bandages and apples, that he was gone less than half a minute. They all piled into the baron's largest limo, with the overflow being carried in the police car, and headed for the observatory.

Janet contrived to sit next to her husband (just as, she was not too preoccupied to notice, Karin and Paul had managed to sit together), but for all the good it did her, she might have been sitting next to a bolster.

It was, in fact, worse than that, because a bolster would at least have kept his mouth shut. About every thirty seconds, Ron would make a fist and whisper, "Of course!"

or, "We should have seen that!" or, "I ought to get somebody to kick me in the ass!"

He wouldn't, Janet thought, have to look outside the family for a volunteer.

When she asked him for a little hint about what this was all about, he said, "Shh, honey, I'm trying to catch up with the old man, and I don't have much time."

So now, he apparently had caught up with the Professor, and they were exchanging intelligent looks, while Janet sat there and stewed. What made it worse was that she wasn't even sure what she was angry about.

She supposed she resented the whole thing's being so goddam *stereotypical*. Less than an hour ago, the Professor had been telling her she'd put her finger on a vital aspect of the case. Swell. She not only didn't know what was so vital about it, she wasn't even sure which finger.

Ron, meantime, had spent this whole trip making connections, watching clues link up like replicating DNA in his mind, until he had the whole organism of the crime complete.

She'd been fighting clichés like "women-are-intuitive-men-are-logical" all her life, and it bothered her that a jerk who believed that could point at her and Ron for evidence.

Then, as she often did, she kidded herself out of it. If that flash of Ron's, even guided by the Professor the way it had been, wasn't intuitive, she didn't know what intuition was. The rest was practice and training.

Which the Professor refused to give her, not because she was a woman, but because she was "too old." Another prejudice she had to fight.

She would, she decided, show them. If the training couldn't be systematic, she'd watch Ron and the Professor, and steal it where she could. In the meantime, she'd continue to contribute what she could as part of the team. But someday, she'd show them. Maybe not the next case, or the one after that, but sometime soon, Janet Higgins would get to the solution of a case the same time as Ron. Maybe even the same time as Benedetti. If fate and love had led her to this kind of life, then by God, she would make it her business to do it right.

The cable car bumped to a halt. The policemen opened the door. Diderot stayed inside; Marx stationed himself outside the door, giving the passengers a helping hand and a sour look as they stepped down.

26

Ron sat in the front row in case the Professor needed him. They were in the observatory's small auditorium/press briefing room, which, according to Karin Tebner, had seen a lot of use in the early, happy days of OSI, right after Hans Goetz had spotted the supernova.

Ron was somewhat surprised to discover, when Karin had let them in with her key, that a bunch of astronomers were in fact on duty tonight. He realized now that he shouldn't have been. Murders were a lot more common than supernovae. Generations of astronomers had lived and died without seeing any of the latter. These guys weren't going to miss the chance.

And there was something comforting, Ron supposed, about the idea of watching, as a new phenomenon, a catastrophe that occurred a long time ago, in a galaxy far, far away. It was sure a lot more comforting than being stuck in the middle of a catastrophe here, now.

A lot of noncomforting thoughts were chasing each other through Ron's head. He had, he believed, a fairly good idea of what the killer had been up to, and why, thanks to the Professor's hint. He even knew what the apples were for.

Unfortunately, Benedetti had neglected to drop any hints about what *he* was up to. For instance, Ron didn't even know what the hell they were up at the observatory for.

He sighed. The only thing to do was try to hang onto the old man's coattails and keep running until you got there. Trust in the Professor and in luck.

Luck. For example, Ron would bet francs to a stale brioche that Benedetti had had no idea there was an auditorium or any other room large enough to hold his "guests" when he planned to come up here. He not only found one, he found one with a lectern, so he could really give it to the class right.

The metaphor fit. Romanescu, Frau Goetz, the baron, all of them, were settling into seats on the raised tiers of the room like students who'd cut too many classes about to face a final exam.

Ron supposed it was natural for them to be nervous, but the only ones who were likely to be called on to recite were Ron himself, and the killer.

The Professor had a few last words with Diderot, then mounted the small stage and stood at the lectern.

"For over a month," the old man began, "this town has been terrorized by a killer who has, by mutual consent, come to be known as 'the Werewolf.'

"This Werewolf has taken three lives. He has, for all practical purposes, destroyed the Olympique Scientifique Internationale, despite the laudable devotion shown by the astronomers working here tonight. He has reduced this place, both its citizens and its visitors, to a state of terror, be it supernatural or otherwise."

"Don't forget the attack on Dr. Romanescu," Karin Tebner said.

Benedetti smiled. "I promise you, I shall not forget it."

He nodded at the Romanian, who nodded back.

"I must confess to a shameful slowness. If I had seen the key clue when it was first presented to me, I could have brought the killer to heel in a matter of hours. In that case, Dr. Jacky Spaak would still be alive."

The old man gave a sad little shrug. "I grieve. But we are all human, eh? If we could do what we wished at the earliest possible opportunity, life would be a simple thing.

"But it is best to begin at the beginning. And a murder investigation almost always begins with the motive. But in this case, we must seek a something beyond a motive for murder."

"This should be educational," Marx snarled.

Benedetti sighed. "I weary of you, Monsieur Marx. Don't you think it is time to drop your impersonation?"

Marx drew back as though he'd been struck. Diderot pulled out a truncheon from his pocket. Ron jumped to his feet. He headed in the Alsatian's general direction, but he kept his face on the Professor.

"Him?" he demanded. *"He's* the killer?"

"No, no. Sit down, *amico.* Marx has his secrets, but he is not the killer. Put your club away, Monsieur Diderot. You will not have to suffer the indignity of having to arrest a brother police officer for these killings. For two reasons. First, he is not the killer. Second, because he is not a police officer."

Diderot was shocked. "But his papers—I checked with the Sûreté—"

"And the Sûreté told you, with great reluctance, and no little anger, what they had been ordered to tell you. That Marx had been sent to replace the murdered Captain de Blois."

Benedetti looked down at Marx. "I can see you planning some internal security probe, even now, Monsieur

Marx. It is not necessary. The head of your organization is a friend of mine. When I presented my suspicions to him over the telephone earlier, he confirmed them."

The baron was confused. "Organization? What organization?"

"DST," Marx said. "Direction de la Surveillance du Territoire. It was thought best, after the second murder, that we have a man on the scene, you see."

Ron looked at him, and saw a completely different man. The hostility was gone. In its place was a man with the air of someone who's just shot a bad round of golf, and is being a good sport about being stuck with the drinks.

"Who thought it best?" the baron demanded. His face was growing redder by the second. "When I tried to begin OSI, the government cautioned me against spies, yes! And I listened to them, used their safeguards to ensure only bona fide scientists came to OSI. And what do I find now? I, Pierre, Baron du Benac, am being spied upon by *France!* I should have at least been told! After all that has befallen, this is the worst—to be suspected by my country of harboring its enemies!"

"You shouldn't take it personally, baron," Marx said. He seemed genuinely concerned. "It's just the way things are done, these days."

"That," Benedetti said, "is all too true. It was done the way things are so often done, these days. Sloppily. You depended on the excellence of your papers to see you through, but it was obvious to see you were no policeman. Especially not one with such a high rank in an organization the like of the Sûreté. There was a time when the DST recruited policemen to its ranks; now like many other intelligence organizations, it contents itself with bright young

things from college campuses. You might have studied police procedure, you know."

Marx shrugged. "No time."

"Cigarettes at the crime scene!" Diderot said. His tone
was the tone of a man vindicated.

"Concentrating on one suspect virtually to the exclu-
sion of everything else," Ron said. "I'd wondered about
that. What was it, raging hormones, or did you think Dr.
Tebner was actually up to something?"

Marx looked at the Professor. "I wonder," he said, "if
you told my superior just how much of our dirty laundry
you intended to wash in public."

He turned to Ron. "To answer your question, Karin is
a charming woman, but I have a wife and family, and my
hormones, as you so charmingly put it, are well taken care
of. Dr. Tebner was singled out for my preliminary attention
because she was involved in the case, and because as a graduate student in 1984, she circulated a petition detrimental to
the interests of the Republic of France."

"I did *what?*" Karin said.

Marx spread his hands as if in apology. "That was my
information."

"You mean when I protested the sinking of an un-
armed Greenpeace boat by the French Navy? Sinking un-
armed environmentalists is *in* the interests of the Republic
of France?"

Levesque muttered, "It is *not,*" and took a grip on
Karin's hand. Ron saw it and smiled.

Benedetti cleared his throat. He had a way of com-
manding attention.

"You might have carried on your imposture in spite of
all this, if you hadn't been so damnably hostile. No police-

man would last a month with an attitude such as you have been affecting. A tough man is not a boor. You must have formulated your ideas of criminal investigation from the same novels as poor Dr. Spaak did."

Marx half smiled, and shrugged again. Ron decided he liked the man better as a snarling pain in the ass than he did as a graceful and unconcerned loser. At least the hostile Marx had seemed to care about something.

"It is always good," Benedetti said, "to clear away the distractions. I regret exposing you to so many, but I cannot do what I must do under your consistent sniping, and you proved impervious to hints. Have you anything further to contribute to the matter at hand?"

Marx was bland. "Not at all. I simply repeat what I have already said—this should be educational."

"I hope it will prove so for all of us."

Benedetti looked around the room to make sure he had everybody's attention. It was the kind of gesture Ron always thought the old man could do without. He'd dropped one little bombshell on Marx, just to show he meant business. He knew they weren't going to let their attention wander, and they knew he knew it, so all this theatricality was wasted. It was hard to argue with the results, but Ron had a natural tendency to want to simplify things. He also had a tendency to start to lose interest once the killer was identified. It would be a big mistake to let that happen now. This baby was dangerous, and was likely to go on being dangerous, despite appearances.

"As I was saying," the Professor went on, "we come to the question of motive. Perhaps I should elaborate. The other two components of the solution to a crime are largely useless to us here. Opportunity excludes virtually no one. This was a gathering of honor, not a summer camp. No one's movements were monitored, and no one was stopped entering or leaving the town. The fact that Monsieur Marx, for example, was not even *in* the town of Mont-St.-Denis when the first two murders occurred means nothing. He could have come and gone with no one the wiser. Alibis, and there are several in this case, are worth slightly more, but not much. While they may clear this person or that one (and we must remember that alibis can be faked and frequently are) this person's or that person's alibi does nothing to advance us toward the truth.

"Means is of even less help than opportunity, for the means were at hand. The murderer struck by crushing or tearing throats, and for a killer like that, every glass bottle is a potential murder weapon. The world is full of jagged objects.

"And so at last, we are back where I began. Looking for a motive. Searching for a motive beyond the simple motive for murder."

"Why do you say that?" Frau Goetz asked. "What can be beyond murder?"

"There are many things, madame," he said sadly. "And neither I as an Italian nor you as a German can ever decently forget what they are. Those things are conquest, and genocide, and the destruction of freedom, and the stifling of the human spirit. In essence, Frau Goetz, the notion, whether held by an individual or spread throughout society, that somehow it is permissible to dispose of the lives of others to suit one's own ends.

"Our countries once thought that way. Other countries have until recently. Some do today. I doubt the killer we seek has ever thought in any other manner.

"But that is not what I meant by seeking a motive beyond murder, either."

By now Ron Gentry would have interrupted any other speaker in the world, saying, "Well, what the hell *do* you mean?"

It wasn't as if Benedetti wasn't giving the rest of the crowd a chance to do it, either. The old man waited a good five seconds before he went on.

"What I mean is, *Why has the killer chosen to be a Werewolf?*"

The members of the audience showed puzzled looks to each other. Most had never thought of things that way. Ron knew one was faking.

"If one maintains," the Professor said, "as I have from the beginning, that these are *not* the random crimes of a madman, then one must answer that question above all others. The very conditions that render the questions of opportunity and means no help tell us that there was a large number of alternative methods to have committed each crime. A gun, a knife, a bludgeon at random intervals, and these murders might never even have been connected.

"So why the viciousness of the attacks? Why strike during the full moon, or near it? Dr. Higgins," he said, and Janet jumped.

"Yes, Professor."

"You have made a survey of the literature of the mental disease known as lycanthropism?"

"Briefly, yes."

"These people believe they turn into wolves?"

"Yes, Professor. Some of them drop to all fours and kill and eat animals."

"Eat them. *Va bène.* Do they restrict their activities to the time of the full moon?"

"No, Professor. Virtually never."

"Then whatever triggers these people in their were-wolflike behavior, it is not the moon?"

"That's correct." Janet was getting better at this.

"I believe, then, we may assume it is not the moon that is triggering the attacks. And yet—"

Again the long pause. This time, somebody bit. Diderot said, "And yet what, Professor?"

"And yet, mystical as it may sound, part of the solution of this case does lie in the heavens."

27

"All we need do, to start, is to find the crater Clavius on the surface of the moon," Benedetti said. He gestured toward the telescope.

Karin Tebner began to step forward. It would be a relief to be able to do *something*. Right now, she didn't know whether to slap Samuel Marx's face (although Professor Benedetti had already done a fairly good symbolic job of that), feel like an idiot for letting the man use her—even to the (thank God) limited extent he had—or just enjoy the feeling she got from being close to Paul Levesque. She ought to slap *his* face, for waiting so long to talk to her. She'd been attracted to *him* since the opening ceremonies, too.

So many conflicting emotions made it almost impossible to sit or stand still, and finding Clavius was something she could do since she was ten years old.

But Benedetti held up a hand to stop her. "Thank you, Dr. Tebner," he said, "but I believe Dr. Romanescu should do the honors." He gave a little grin. "Seniority, you know."

Poor Dr. Romanescu stood against the wall with a bewildered look on his face.

Benedetti had moved everyone from the auditorium to the observatory proper to look for the killer in the heavens, whatever that meant. Karin was delighted to note that the Professor did not intend to dispossess her colleagues from the main reflector. The nova was a lot harder to find than Clavius.

Fortunately, Benedetti was content to lead everyone into what Karin liked to think of as the hobby room. This was an annex of the observatory in which the baron had thoughtfully provided six extremely good backyard-type serious-amateur telescopes for visiting dignitaries and journalists to look through without disturbing the real work.

"Dr. Romanescu?" Benedetti said "Please?"

"No, no," the Romanian said. "I yield gladly to Dr. Tebner."

"I insist," Benedetti told him. "Please. Any telescope you choose."

Romanescu was shaking as he walked forward. The poor man was so befuddled, he started trying to pull a focus before he had even moved the shaft, then he tried to move it without unlocking the pivot, and almost knocked the whole three-thousand-dollar toy over.

He looked up with a sad smile. "I'm sorry. I—I can't seem to concentrate. I just . . ."

His voice trickled away. There were a few seconds of embarrassed silence.

"All right, Doctor," Benedetti's voice was gentle. "It's not important any more. Dr. Tebner, would you please attend to it?"

She had the telescope sighted on Clavius, focused, and locked down in fifteen seconds. She could have done it in ten, but she didn't want to make Romanescu feel any worse than he already did.

"Are we supposed to look now at the moon?" the baron asked.

"You may if you like, baron. It is, after all, your telescope."

So they all looked. Even poor Romanescu. Even Benedetti's assistants. Everyone but Benedetti himself. At the
end, Karin took another peek. If the killer's name was up
there, it was beyond her abilities to read it. No wonder
Benedetti hadn't looked.

"Thank you," he said. "Most enlightening. And now, I
think, we should return to the auditorium."

As she followed the crowd, Karin didn't feel the least
bit enlightened. What she felt was creepy. Something was
going on here, something more than the revelation of a
killer, some kind of mind game, and she didn't know the
rules.

It occurred to her that she didn't even know if she was
a spectator or one of the participants, and that made her
feel creepier than ever.

When they got back to the auditorium, they all sat in
the seats they'd had before, like a bunch of school kids.
Benedetti nodded to Ron Gentry, and Gentry picked up a
paper bag he'd been carrying since before they'd left the
château, opened it up, and began to walk around the room
handing out apples.

Karin looked at the apple in her hand, and remembered Janet's husband breathlessly gasping the word as
though it meant something to him. She stole a glance at
Janet, and saw her hefting hers as if she wanted to throw it
at somebody.

"Does everyone have an apple?" Benedetti asked.

Karin half expected the group to speak in unison, saying "Yes, we do, Professor," but there was a simple chorus
of mumbled assent.

"Magnifique," Marx said. "Refreshments."

"Va bène. The apples may be eaten later, if you wish. They are, like so much, the largesse of the baron. But what I wish to use them for now is to allow you to see for yourselves the solution to this case." He touched his bandaged left cheek lightly and smiled. "And I am glad to say you will learn this much less painfully than I."

Benedetti was suddenly serious. "Now, I want you all to be werewolves. The apple is helpless flesh. Claw it."

No one moved.

"Do it!" Benedetti shouted. "Use your nails and rip! One set of clawmarks will suffice."

Marx shrugged and dug into his apple almost clinically. She saw Paul beside her claw at his as though it was Marx's face, which inspired Karin to use her nails on her own. One way or another, all the apples got scratched. When Karin looked up, Ron Gentry was already roaming the room handing out paper towels from the men's room.

"Excellent," the Professor said. "Now look at the marks you have made in the skin of the apple. Do you see the narrow triangle, narrowest at the point at which the skin was broken, then wider as the nails penetrated more deeply, stopping, or perhaps tapering off slightly when they are withdrawn?

"Human nails are not primarily intended for clawing. They do not slice a clean line, like the claws of a cat or an eagle do. Human nails pierce and drag, and they make this characteristic shape. It was a fact I had forgotten, until I attempted to shave this afternoon. Ronald, will you help me?"

Ron Gentry joined the Professor at the podium. He loosened the old man's bandage, then pulled it off. There were dark red marks on the old man's nut-brown face, with whiskers bristling between them. Even from here, Karin could see the triangular shape of the wounds.

"I angered a person this morning, you see," Benedetti said, "and got myself scratched. The person was facing me, and scratched with the right hand. Therefore, the scratches are on my left cheek, with the wide end foremost.

"When I saw that in the mirror, I remembered where I had seen marks like that before. And a very few seconds later, I saw all there was to see.

"If any of you would like a closer look, you are welcome to approach me."

Benedetti sent a look like a flying piece of steel into the audience.

"Or perhaps," he went on, "Dr. Romanescu would oblige us by revealing his left cheek."

Romanescu shouted, "No!" He jumped to his feet and began clambering over seats, trying to get to the exit. He showed no signs of being the doddering old man he had seemed at the telescope.

Ron Gentry tried to catch him, but only succeeded in tearing the collar from the back of the man's jacket. That slowed him down enough for Diderot and Marx to get to the doorway ahead of him. Faced with the guns of the two Frenchmen, Romanescu stopped.

"Well, I'm good for something after all, am I not, Professor?" Marx said brightly. Benedetti ignored him.

Diderot spun the Romanian around to put handcuffs on him. Romanescu's face wore a look of purest hate.

"There is your Werewolf," Benedetti said.

28

Etienne Diderot was a resort-town cop, not a mastermind. He had a long way to go to catch up with the great Professor Niccolo Benedetti. But he knew that when a mild-mannered old man like Romanescu turns into a snarling athlete bent on escape at the first accusation, somebody was onto something.

Diderot brought his prisoner before Benedetti. He reached out to the man's left cheek and pulled the bandage loose. After a month, the scratches were nearly healed, but one could still discern the characteristic triangular shape, with the wide part closest the front. Diderot fondly hoped he would soon be allowed to know what significance that held.

"It wasn't necessary to do that, Monsieur Diderot," the Professor told him.

Diderot felt indignant. "The man was fleeing. He had to be caught."

Benedetti was patient. "Yes, I understand that. It was not, however, necessary to pull off the bandage. You have the slides, have you not?"

"The slides?"

"The photographic transparencies you showed to my associates and me on our arrival. When I telephoned you I asked you to bring them with you."

"Oh," Diderot said. He was beginning to get irritated with himself. He did not consider himself a stupid man, but the rapid string of revelations was making him *feel* stupid. "Yes. We have brought those."

"Excellent," Benedetti told him. "I believe this room has a projection booth. Perhaps the useful Monsieur Marx can be dispatched there to show the slides. Or one particular slide."

It was all arranged in less than two minutes. Diderot had rearranged the handcuffs so that his prisoner was chained to his seat, and sat next to him. The crowd had been calmed, the room darkened. Marx rapidly shuffled through the evidence slides.

"Stop!" Benedetti said. "There it is. There is the clue that should have led me to the identity of the Werewolf before he had even chosen the name.

"Because those marks show incontrovertibly that whoever made those marks on Romanescu's cheek was *facing* him. But what was the story he told the police? That he had been taking a walk when a *madman attacked him from behind*. He saw nothing, except 'a man in brown' fleeing the scene, and even that he was vague about.

"But that story, my friends, was the work of a brilliant mind, operating under pressure. At one stroke, it accounted for the marks on his cheek; it moved Romanescu directly into the class of 'potential victims' rather than of suspects. And he began to lay the groundwork for a chimera, an illusionary entity that could be blamed for the murder, if need be—the 'man in brown.' All this, before the first body was even discovered."

"I can hardly believe this." The baron was wringing his hands. "Dr. Romanescu, how can this have happened? After all you went through, when you were finally free—

why did you kill Dr. Goetz? Did you not know he was the one who insisted you be invited in the first place?"

Romanescu sat and said nothing. There was the suggestion of a smile on his face.

"I believe," the Professor said, "you give the man the wrong honorific. It's not 'Doctor' Romanescu, is it?"

Just as he had at that first briefing session, Diderot saw Benedetti launch a blind pass to young Gentry.

"My colleague will elaborate," the Professor said. "Won't you, Ronald?"

"Of course, Professor," Ron said. Ron was ready for him, this time. "I think I can help clear things up if I poll the crowd on a couple of questions. First, Baron, I noticed you addressed your question to Romanescu in English."

"I always have," the baron said. "We all have."

"I think you're right," Ron said. He addressed the whole group. "Anybody know anything different? Has anyone ever addressed a word in French to Romanescu and gotten an answer? Think hard, now. Anybody ever hear him speak a word of French?"

There was a general shaking of heads.

"Neither have I," Ron said. "The prefect will remember the day Romanescu tried to 'flee' town—in reality, just calling attention to the werewolf idea. Why was I able to persuade him to come back after you weren't? Because I spoke English. The prefect spoke French—Romanescu simply didn't *understand* him. And this is supposed to be a man whose official biography says he *taught* at a French university for several years before he fell out of favor with the Romanian government, was ordered to return, and was placed under house arrest.

"I mean, I know it's been a long time, but he can't have been in France for a couple of years and not have learned *anything*. I've been here less than a week—"

"Seems longer," Janet mumbled so only Ron could hear.

He suppressed a smile and went on. "—and *I've* learned enough French to tell a taxi driver where to go. Romanescu had to have the hotel clerk do it for him.

"No, I think our friend here is someone who's never been in France before. I think he's learned a good few months' worth of the language in the time he's been here. But he found himself facing an interesting problem. If he used the French he'd picked up since OSI began, he might remind someone that he ought to be considerably more fluent than he is. No, safer to get by with no French at all, and possible because so many people here speak English."

"Sacrebleu!" said the man in the handcuffs. He was enjoying this. Ron wondered if this was just bravado or what. It was too bad, Ron decided, that it hadn't been Marx who'd gotten the handcuffs on Romanescu. Those two deserved each other.

"Now about that demonstration with the telescope earlier. That wasn't—"

"He couldn't find Clavius," Karin Tebner said. "I felt so sorry for him, because he had been a great astronomer, and now he couldn't even find Clavius."

Ron nodded. "Now you know that Clavius had nothing to do with it. That the Professor didn't give a *damn* about Clavius."

Ron could say that now, of course. What he couldn't forget was the way his brain did twisting somersaults when the Professor had first come up with this, trying to decide what the hell a crater on the moon had to do with murders in the here and now.

"The idea was for you to see that this man—as Dr. Tebner said, a great astronomer—*didn't even know how to use a simple telescope* to find one of the most prominent features on the moon.

"How am I doing, Maestro?"

"Excellent," the old man said. "Please continue."

Ron grinned at the old man for a change. "I had no intention of stopping." Again, he addressed the audience. "The question now was, since he obviously wasn't Dr. Ion Romanescu, noted astronomer, who was he?

"As the Professor said, we've been applying the wrong honorific. I forget what the right one was." He turned to the prisoner. "What was it? Major? Colonel? We can look it up."

"I say nothing. I admit nothing. I will trust to French law."

Ron caught a glimpse of the Professor. For some reason the old man was grinning almost wide enough to make his cheek bleed again. Which reminded him that the Professor's bandage had yet to be replaced. That was all he needed, something else to worry about.

"Fine," Ron said. "We'll look it up. Some of you may not know this, but the brother I mentioned earlier, the one who caused the disgrace and arrest of Ion Romanescu so many years ago, was an officer in the Romanian secret police, in tight with the recently deposed Ceausescu regime. He was a wanted man when Ceausescu fell, hunted assiduously until his body was found among those of rioters and Ceausescu's guards outside a government building.

"That's the story, anyway. I think it was the astronomer's body that was found, dumped there by his brother, who assumed his identity. Maybe even identified the body for the new government, huh? Then waited on tenterhooks for some chance to get out of Romania. OSI must have seemed like a gift from the angels. Not only would it get you out of Romania, where a slip at any moment could put you in front of a summary firing squad, it put you in a position to stay permanently in the West."

"I say nothing. I admit nothing."

Marx, the spy, formerly Captain Marx, cleared his throat. "I—uh—think you are forgetting something."

"I forget nothing," Benedetti said.

"Fingerprints," Marx said. "The fingerprints Diderot and de Blois had collected and were matching. I was there when Reggiani, the greatest fingerprint man in Europe, went over them. *That* Italian genius said categorically there was no impostor at the Olympique Scientifique Internationale."

"That Italian genius," Benedetti echoed, "overstepped the bounds of his expertise. All Signor Reggiani could truthfully say is that the fingerprints he was given to examine matched. That is all. That he said more one must attribute to the regrettable weakness of some of my countrymen for the theatrical gesture."

Ron choked back a laugh; so did Janet. Nobody else bothered. The Professor pretended not to notice.

"The fingerprints *did* match," the old man went on. "That is the whole point."

"What whole point?" Marx asked.

"The point that unlike you, dear 'Captain,' our killer *does* think like a policeman. Even in totalitarian regimes, there is a certain amount of professionalism attached to the job. Even Mussolini's thugs, with whom I had some experience as a young man, were aware of the *concept* of evidence, and liked to find it, as long it didn't interfere with their use of the truncheon.

"And those things, the fact of the imposture, and the background of the impostor, explain so much. They answer almost all the questions remaining.

"It answers Frau Goetz's questions about why her husband, about whom no bad word has ever been heard that was not planted by *you,* Monsieur Marx, was killed. Quite simply, Dr. Goetz was killed because he was too good a man. A more self-centered man, especially one who was in charge of a section of OSI, *especially* one who had made a rare and spectacular discovery, would not have spent time worrying about a contemporary who didn't seem to be able to run the simplest equipment any more. That man would have ignored the incompetence and gotten on with his own work, much to the false Dr. Romanescu's delight.

"But Hans Goetz *cared.* It was he who had arranged for the invitation to Romanescu in the first place. And undoubtedly he was there with sympathy, advice, offers of help. Eventually, he must have seen something that caused suspicion even in a mind as generous as his.

"Still, he does not act. He waits until the inevitable time everyone is off from work, and away from the observatory, and arranges a secret late-night walk. Perhaps this impostor is a poor refugee. Perhaps Hans Goetz can still be of help.

"Of course, the impostor is a killer, and Hans Goetz is a deadly danger. Romanescu reaches for his throat—in the struggle, fighting desperately to his last breath, Goetz claws Romanescu across the cheek.

He looked at the Romanian. "How delightful you must have found it to tell me—in perfect truthfulness—

how frightened you were during that first attack. You weren't frightened *by* it, as I was meant to believe; you were frightened into making it, by Dr. Goetz's suspicions.

"And this answers your question, as well, Dr. Tebner. Why was the body held in the flames of the torch in the Place du Science? Very simple. The policeman's mind knows that not only is he standing there with a scratched cheek, but that *particles of his flesh are under the dead man's fingernails.* That evidence must be obliterated. A simple crime of convenience must become an act of horror so great it overwhelms rational thought. One victim and one killer must become one victim and one near-victim of some bestial fiend. So the body goes into the fire, to burn the flesh of both the killer and the victim. And Romanescu goes into the police station with his story of a vicious attack—we have all seen tonight what a good actor he is—and in that moment, the Werewolf is born."

29

There was silence for a minute or so, broken only by soft sobs from Frau Goetz.

"I am sorry, madam," the Professor said softly. "In the end, I think you will find it better to know the truth."

The old man went on to outline the second murder. Ron had spent most of the trip up on the cable car working it out for himself.

Romanescu had made a mistake. Two mistakes, really. He had underestimated the uproar the murder would cause, maybe because of his lifelong immersion in a terrorist state. And, figuring he'd be safe with Goetz gone, he had gone back to "work."

Ron could almost feel the pressure mounting on the man, coming up here night after night, while down below Diderot and de Blois were doing their good solid job of police work. Then came the universal fingerprint canvass. Romanescu fights panic—he knows what's coming next. He knows they'll wire back to Bucharest for his brother's prints, and he knows they won't match.

But he doesn't dare *do* anything about it until there's a night off, and for the eyeball astronomers, nights off come once a month, in bunches.

When the time comes, it's almost too late. The replies are in; de Blois is going to go over them that very night.

"De Blois must be stopped," the Professor said, paralleling Ron's thoughts. "Romanescu watches the police station, sees that de Blois is there with one other officer. That makes it simple. He goes a block or two away, and breaks the window of a jewelry store. Perhaps he retrieves a chunk of broken glass; perhaps he has a weapon of his own.

"He returns to the police station, waits for the officer to leave to investigate the break-in, then enters. Captain de Blois fears nothing from this man. Too bad for him. Romanescu stuns him with a blow, finds the report from Romania among the stack of papers, and replaces it with a counterfeit he has prepared, with his own, matching fingerprints on it. He then places de Blois across the desk, and butchers him.

"Notice, please. Who but a policeman would be able to counterfeit a *fingerprint form?* Of course, he knew the form itself would get no intense scrutiny—everyone would be concentrating on the prints themselves. Another brilliant move under pressure. I congratulate you."

"I say nothing," the prisoner said. "I admit nothing." Ron was about ready to go up and smack him.

If he weren't such a bastard, Ron could have almost sympathized with him. After he'd killed de Blois, Romanescu found that he'd made the place much, much too hot. The baron was going to fly this hotshot Benedetti in from the States, and they'd heard of him even beyond the Iron Curtain.

Romanescu had three priorities. One, not to have to be a "scientist" anymore. Two, to confuse things so badly no one would ever uncover the truth. Three, to get the hell out of Mont-St.-Denis.

"He went to work the day I arrived," the Professor said, "with that clumsy flight—in a taxicab!—down the mountain, his feigning of insanity, the talk of werewolves, and a death coming with the next full moon.

"A few days in the hospital, and he was a new man. But he was a new man who was no longer expected to go to the observatory. Better yet, he was ensconced in the baron's château, where he could learn if we were getting close to anything.

"But this brilliant move gave rise to another complication. The notion of the Werewolf took hold, however subtly, among the scientists. They began to neglect their work and turn their minds to murder, led, of course, by Jacky Spaak, who was killed by his own romantic nature."

"Why was Spaak killed?" Levesque wanted to know. "It all seemed so unnecessary."

"It wasn't necessary," the Professor said. "It was *convenient.* When faced with evil, one must imagine the values of the evil one. Remember, Romanescu wanted nothing in the world as much as he wanted OSI to break up and its participants to scatter. It was, by then, on the brink. One more murder would do it, he reasoned. The question was, could he commit one safely?

"Yes, he could. He couldn't leave the château, or rather, it wouldn't be prudent to do so. But his assessment of the would-be private eye Jacky Spaak told him that Spaak could be induced to come to him."

Benedetti looked at the Romanian. "What did you promise him? What you 'really' saw the night Goetz was killed? Did you tell him you felt you could trust him because he was a fellow scientist?"

"I say nothing."

"Yes, and admit nothing, I know. It doesn't matter. I can see it as plainly as if I were there. You arranged a midnight rendezvous near the château fence, nearest the

guest wing. You slid down a sheet from your first-floor
window, after letting us all think how brave you were to
leave it open and forfeit the internal alarm. You went to the
gardener's shed and 'borrowed' a three-pronged cultivator
and a rake handle and taped the one to the other until you
had what in effect was a five-foot pole with a claw.

"Then you crouched in the darkness and waited for
him to come. When he arrived, you had him bend close to
the fence, then raked up at him between the bars with your
weapon. You tore his throat and left him for dead. You
headed back for the house.

"I assume you were rather proud of yourself. You'd
brought the Werewolf to the baron's doorstep, and hadn't
gotten a drop of blood on you. A *little* past the full moon,
but that couldn't be helped.

"But you may have congratulated yourself too soon.
Because before you could get back to the house, the baker
came along, found the body, stumbled into the fence and set
off the alarm. You had time only to take your weapon apart
and clamber back into your room before my assistant arrived and pounded on your door. You put on another of
your award-winning performances in delaying him outside
the door while you put the sheet back on the bed.

"You put on another act the next day, when I discovered you retrieving the parts of your weapon (Mr. Gentry
had actually stepped on one the night before), and washing
the blood off them before my very eyes. You were feeling
confident, then—you had the audacity to ask *me* if I would
arrange for you to come to the United States!

"But you made another mistake. In the semidarkness
of the gardener's shed, you put the cultivator and the handle back *precisely* where they belonged without a moment's

hesitation. You knew where they went because you had taken them.

"And that, I believe, explains everything. M. Diderot, take him away. I will spend my hour alone with him at the jail. For now, the sight of him makes me—"

Romanescu's voice was loud and strong. No one had heard anything like it from him before. It was the voice of a man much younger than the seventy Ion Romanescu had claimed. They stopped and listened.

"I say nothing," he began, "except this: How long do you expect me to be in jail? You have told a story, Professor Benedetti, but if you had been listening carefully, you would have heard yourself describe how all the evidence has been destroyed or washed clean or never existed in the first place. In the West, there is no truncheon; there is only this precious evidence. I do not think a French court will convict me."

Benedetti walked up to the man and laughed out loud, something he rarely did. He laughed for a long time. Finally he said, "You may never see the inside of a French court."

"Now see here," Diderot began.

Benedetti ignored him. "It is a matter of utter indifference to me; it rests entirely in your hands."

"What does that mean?" Diderot demanded.

Marx smiled. He smiled so wide he had to take the cigarette from his mouth. *"Très bien,* Professor. I see. You simply have the prefect send another wire to Bucharest . . ."

". . . and this time have them send the fingerprints of Romanescu's brother, the secret policeman. Precisely," Benedetti said. He looked the prisoner in the eye. "Then, you are simply repatriated to the new government of Romania, who, I am sure, will have a warm welcome for you, and you need not trouble yourself at all about French justice."

Romanescu's face fell like a balloon with a slow leak. His eyes fell from Benedetti's. He tried to raise them again to meet the Professor's gaze, but failed.

"Take him to headquarters, Monsieur Diderot," the Professor said. "And call ahead for a stenographer. I believe you'll be taking a confession."

30

"My favorite part of the whole thing, Maestro, was after it was all over, when Frau Goetz gave Marx that rap across the mouth, then came over and hung a big kiss on you."

Professor Benedetti rubbed his mouth, as though to wipe off the memory of the kiss. Or to rub it in, Karin thought.

They were on an Air France 747 heading back to New York. When Karin had run into the Professor's party in the gate lounge, they had arranged to sit together. First class, and the baron was paying.

"At least he has a fighting chance to save his empire now," Janet said.

"You think so?" her husband asked.

Janet nodded. "The Professor delivered the goods, and the baron is a hero, now."

"And loving it," Ron said. "I guess the secret to being a billionaire is not letting catastrophes get you down. When he said good-bye, he was getting all moony-eyed—sorry, bad choice of words—he expressed enthusiasm over the idea of an international convocation of master detectives. He was just asking the Professor if he was acquainted with this Armenian guy who works out of Philadelphia when we took off. It was the first time I've ever seen the Professor run."

"I did not run. And, Ronald, do I have to tell you, of all people, that I am a philosopher and not a detective?"

"You haven't mentioned your hour with Romanescu," Janet said.

"Bah. Love of power and contempt for others. Quite banal. It's amazing the horrible results one can cause with such basic and uncomplicated evil impulses." The Professor pursed his lips for a moment. *"Va bène.* And perhaps that is not such a trivial insight. We shall see."

"You can read a paper on it at the baron's convocation," Ron suggested.

"I am going to no convocations. I did nothing great on this case."

"I think it was pretty wonderful," Karin said.

Benedetti leaned over to talk to her. "Young lady, I had not the slightest inkling of the truth until a chance event rubbed my nose—or at least my cheek—in it. And by then, it was nearly too late. I have come as close to failure as I ever hope to come."

"Does this mean I have to give the money back?" Ron asked. Janet slapped his arm.

"But you did work it out, in time, Professor," Karin said. "Isn't that what counts?"

"Your subconscious had it pegged, Maestro. That last painting. The *three* faces; a double imposture. The secret policeman pretending to be the astronomer pretending to be a werewolf. Brilliant. Where did the baron say he was going to hang it?"

Benedetti just grunted. Janet decided to change the subject. "Karin, I didn't expect to see you heading to the States so soon. You and Paul looked as if you were starting something."

"I'm going back," she said, and she could feel herself blush as she said it. "In a month. Paul said he has to plunge into saving the baron's business holdings, and won't be able to come up for air for a month. It will give me a chance to clean things up in New Mexico."

"Are you going to get married?"

"That," Karin said firmly, "has not yet come up. But there is a beautiful new observatory up there, and somebody has to run it. . . ."

"The way to a woman's heart," Ron said, "is through her career."

But Karin didn't want to talk about herself. Instead, she turned and looked out the window, and there it was, lopsided-round and yellow, with parallax making it look as though it was following them home.

"The moon," she said. Then she turned back to face her companions. "Professor! The moon!"

"What about it?" the old man said.

"That's what I want to know. What about it? The whole idea of the Werewolf was Romanescu's attempt to break up OSI. But that wouldn't have worked unless the murders, at least the first two, had been committed during the full moon."

"That is a reasonable assumption."

"Was it just a coincidence, then?"

"Oh, no. Cause and effect."

"Cause and effect? You mean, somehow, the moon made Romanescu commit these murders?"

"Of course not. I'm sure that in a long life of evil he has killed people under any condition imaginable. But the moon dictated the *timing* of his murders. Dictated to Dr. Goetz in the first instance, and to Romanescu in the second.

You, my dear, should understand this better than anyone. Too much light? Bad seeing conditions?"

And Benedetti smiled for the first time in a long time. "You see, this was perhaps the first werewolf in history to strike during the full moon simply because it was his night off."